I0627700

KAYONGA'S DECISION AND OTHER STORIES

KAYONGA'S DECISION AND OTHER STORIES

DAVE CREEK

Hydra Publications

Copyright © 2021 by Dave Creek

All rights reserved.

No part of this book may be reproduced in any form or by any electronic or mechanical means, including information storage and retrieval systems, without written permission from the author, except for the use of brief quotations in a book review.

ISBN: 978-1-948374-65-1

First Edition

Hydra Publications

Goshen, Kentucky 40026

www.hydrapublications.com

Praise for Dave Creek

"One of the best ways to get a fix of otherness is with expertly-conceived and well-depicted aliens . . . That's why it's such a joy to find an author who can do it well.

"Dave Creek is one of those authors."

-- Don Sakers, ANALOG SCIENCE FICTION

"The world building is most impressive . . . I see too few writers willing to take the trouble to do it these days."

-- Dr. Stanley Schmidt, former editor, ANALOG SCIENCE FICTION

"*The Unmoving Stars* is a gripping tale of humans fighting against time and vast interstellar distances to return home."

-- Jason Sanford, two-time Nebula Award finalist

Good hard science fiction is in short supply these days. I recommend this book (*The Human Equations*) as a fast and entertaining read for the science fiction fan."

-- Jason Sizemore, editor, APEX MAGAZINE

Contents

Also by Dave Creek

Hydra books by Dave Creek:

A GLIMPSE OF SPLENDOR (collection)

SOME DISTANT SHORE

THE HUMAN EQUATIONS (collection)

TRAJECTORIES (editor)

CHANDA'S AWAKENING

ALL HUMAN THINGS

PUBLISHING HISTORY

"Introduction," by Jack McDevitt, copyright 2021 by Cryptic, Inc.

"The Dominant Heart Begins to Race" appeared in ANALOG, May/June 2019.

Beyond Human Measure" appeared in AMAZING STORIES, Fall 2018. Copyright 2018 by Dave Creek.

"Finding Chidera" appeared in DYSTOPIAN EXPRESS. Copyright 2016 by Dave Creek.

"Kayonga's Decision" appeared in TOUCHING THE FACE OF THE COSMOS. Copyright 2015 by Dave Creek.

"Shepherding" appeared in PERIHELION SF, April 2015. Copyright 2015 by Dave Creek.

"Silhouettes" appeared in ANALOG, September 2016. Copyright 2016 by Dave Creek.

"A Grand Gesture" appeared in ANALOG, May/June 2017 Copyright 2017 by Dave Creek.

"Short on Thought, Quick on the Trigger" appeared in PERIHELION SF. Copyright 2016 by Dave Creek.

"Sungazers" is original to this volume. Copyright 2021 by Dave Creek

To Susan Sweeney Crum
Loyal Reader

Introduction

by
Jack McDevitt

Introducing a collection of work from a writer who functions at Dave Creek's level is something of a challenge. He's been a regular contributor to ANALOG and other science fiction markets for years. He's written several novels, including *Some Distant Shore*, *The Unmoving Stars*, *Chanda's Awakening*, and *All Human Things*. *Some Distant Shore* and the novella "A Crowd of Stars" have both won the Imadjinn Award.

Like so many from his generation, and from my earlier one, he stood on the deck of the Enterprise with Captain Kirk and Mr. Spock while simultaneously watching us land on the Moon. All of us living in those years who were paying any kind of attention could not have avoided being swept away by the possibilities of the future. Dave was obviously among them.

After we arrived on the Moon, people started talking about going to Mars. Science fiction writers during the fifties expected it to happen within twenty years. We were on our way, baby. No question about it. Anything was possible.

A lot of things did happen. We put the Hubble Telescope in orbit. And we got close-up pictures from automated flybys of the outer solar system. But where manned space flight was concerned, most of it was a disappointment. We sent a flight to Mars. There was nobody on board, but it was nevertheless a spectacular breakthrough, even if it turned out there were no canals. Venus, which had been portrayed by some writers as a jungle world, turned out to be a dismal sunbaked desert. SETI tuned up and started listening to the sky but to this day has heard nothing. We demoted Pluto to a minor planet.

In the end, we've left footprints nowhere except on the Moon.

Spurred on by what had not happened as well as by what had, writers created the interplanetary investigation which they'd expected to witness during their lifetimes. And they hoped to see answers to the big questions: Does life exist else-where? Is there any evidence of intelligence out there? Dave takes on these issues, and obviously enjoys delivering surprises as to how exotic life in other places might be, and the degree to which intelligent creatures might differ from humans. Or possibly resemble us. And how it can get the most well-meaning people into serious trouble.

And other worlds may be different in unexpected ways. We know some gas giants have rings. Is size a requirement? Not in the Dave Creek cosmos. And probably not in ours.

He provides perspectives that are both exhilarating and unnerving: intelligent whales swimming through the Jovian atmosphere, aliens who were forced to evacuate their home world and watch while it collided with a rogue planet. And Manta gliders with wide wings who use ten thousand feet to feed and hunt in concert.

He examines the effects technological adjustments to our bodies may have on the way we live. And the difficulties that may arise when some of us begin settling into homes on orbital habitats. What do we do if we move onto a world with a dazzling ring system but discover the ring system is causing severe ecological damage?

His characters have to make difficult decisions. Do we leave a woman we love to go back to Earth, where we desperately want to live? A couple of us arrive on a world that is now an Earth colony. The original inhabitants are long gone. But they unexpectedly return. They are not malicious but they demand the humans leave. The two groups gradually approach a violent confrontation. Whose side are we on?

A substantial number of possibilities will arise from technological advances. We've already seen how the internet has changed our lives. Dave points out a few other issues that may surface, and while he makes the point that much of it will be good news, he suggests there will be times when it might be smart to keep our heads down.

The stories in *Kayonga's Decision* confront a wide range of issues. But Dave does it with insight and compassion.

Jack McDevitt is the author of the best-selling
Priscilla Hutchins and Alex Benedict novels.
For more information on his work, go to
https://www.jackmcdevitt.com/

Foreword

This is my third short story collection, and within these pages you'll find some familiar series characters including Carrie Molina and Leo Bakri alongside some newer characters who may or may not become regulars in my stories. These tales take place a billion years in the past and over 150 years in the future, on Earth and on far-flung alien worlds.

In addition to the stories reprinted from various magazine and anthology appearances over the years, I've included a tale featuring Carrie Molina that's never appeared anywhere else before.

Enjoy!

The Dominant Heart Begins to Race

The eternal question that many readers ask writers is, "Where do you get your ideas?" The late, great, writer Harlan Ellison used to say he bought a bunch of his ideas for $25 a pop from a guy from Poughkeepsie. Apparently it never occurs to a lot of people that such an answer only pushes the question back one step -- where does the person selling the ideas get them?

That's a question I'll answer regarding "The Dominant Heart Begins to Race" in an afterword, since the explanation could be considered rather spoiler-ific.

I'd like to thank Marianne Dyson and Trent Walters for their invaluable comments and advice that vastly improved this story.

Note: Ytani terms for units of time and distance in this story have been "translated" into English.

———

With each awakening, each resurrection as I think of it, my lifespan shortens. This first thought always floods my

1

consciousness even as the liquid nutrients that have sustained me within the stasis chamber swirl away. My body warms, all my arms and both legs loosen up, both hearts once again beat in rhythm. Despite my own sacrifice in waking up yet again, it pleases me that the ship, the *Shovach*, has found another potential star system for the remnants of my people. The curve of my chamber's transparent cover reflects that pleasure back down toward me in the soft gray glow of my crest.

The chamber's diagnostic systems run through their final examinations of my physical and mental status, making sure no infections, blood clots, or other medical factors endanger me, that my senses have returned to their full functioning, and that the *Shovach's* life-support systems and artificial gravity have started up properly. Diving into stasis, then returning years or centuries later, takes a toll upon the body, and the ship must know that I can function.

I answer the usual questions, yes, I know my name, Draiora, I represent one of the last refugees from the doomed planet Ytani, and the ship has awakened me to examine the latest star system that could provide my people with a new home.

As often happens in these final moments before the chamber opens, my consciousness, unbidden, brings up images of my homeworld, Ytani, and its destruction. I shake my head back and forth, trying to force my attention elsewhere even as the reflection of my crest turns from gray to a brilliant, sad, white, but the result remains the same as with all my other awakenings -- the close approach of the rogue planet Udeni, tidal stresses tearing away my homeworld's crust, cities torn asunder, billions upon billions dying in an instant. Even as my chamber's cover opens upward, my attention remains focused on memories of those two worlds as they collide and begin to merge. I sit up and swing my legs onto the floor, making sure to hold on tight to the edge of the chamber with all four arms, and recall looking back at the remains of two worlds in the process of melding together, magma flowing freely, their atmosphere and volatiles vaporizing into space, lost forever. Images that will continue to haunt me for the rest of my days, no matter how many centuries those days might embrace.

No other planets in our star system existed that could support intelligent life. Our starship *Shovach* accelerated quickly out of the system, until even our sun faded into the distance, one undistinguished star among so many.

I stand, legs wobbly, and take my first tentative steps. This awakening already demands a higher toll, both physical and mental, from me, and it takes longer than usual for me to regain my balance and ability to step forward with confidence. The body only contains so much vitality, and each successive period spent in stasis drains more of that vitality than the previous ones.

All around me stand dozens more stasis chambers containing the other fifty-five Ytani adult individuals the ship may choose to awaken when it arrives at a star system that could contain a possible colony planet. In planning this mission, our best estimates told us that we would certainly find a suitable world to colonize within a few decades, requiring only a few awakenings, probably none of us more than once.

Now we live with that miscalculation. I've awakened nine times so far across several centuries, and ship's records show that others have gone through even more periods of stasis and awakening. Within a few more centuries, none of us may have the vitality we need to continue our explorations and, if we find success, to establish a colony on some yet-unknown world.

Shovach always allows time for the person awakened to recover before having to take action. I need to clean up and have something to eat before I begin my work, but I stop in front of my mentor Rynon's stasis chamber. I look down at her face, her light blue skin nearly translucent as she sleeps. I admire her strong upper arms, which allow her to help in tasks requiring physical strength, and her more slender lower arms, whose skilled hands and fingers have assisted me on countless technical tasks. I also admire the smooth lines of her cheek-bones and the curve of her crest as it sweeps back from her forehead, its color a light tan that reflects no emotion as she sleeps. I ache to see her awake, red eyes alive and piercing, crest able to turn from an exultant gray to angry scarlet in an instant, given the proper provocation. I could easily admire her as more than my mentor, but I dare not think of her in such an inappropriate way.

I wish I had good reason to revive her. I could use my mentor's wise advice. If such a reason existed, though, *Shovach* would have awakened her.

I go to my quarters and indulge in a sono-shower, put on new clothes, and prepare a brief meal of bangh meat and neylynn juice. Then, time to work.

As I enter the primary control room, the ship senses my presence and the walls begin to glow, their familiar hues of blue and green a comfort. Some areas feature mechanical or electronic interfaces upon their walls; others require only a person's touch against living tissue to activate.

An outsider might not find this circular room, only fifteen meters across, very large, given that it operates a starship eleven kilometers long, with a hundred levels, containing the remnants of an entire sentient species. But only eleven thousand fully-grown adults exist here, and most of them sleep the years away. They represent the core population of an eventual colony that will maintain our species. The ship only chooses one of fifty-five of us, including myself, among the eleven thousand to awaken when it detects one or more possible colony planets within a particular star system.

The remainder of our species takes up much less room aboard, existing only as billions of fertilized eggs held in stasis. Potential people. People awaiting their destiny.

A destiny I hope to discover for them, perhaps this very day.

I make my way around the control room, checking ship's systems, expecting all of them to display proper functioning.

But they do not. In fact, several ship's systems have malfunctioned, including most of its decision-making modules. Given that, the ship decided, as it should, to maintain life-support for its inhabitants above all other priorities, with propulsion and other engineering capabilities close behind. But it approaches a new system, and its weakened state intellectually, combined with its inability to gather sufficient data, means it cannot decide whether to slow itself to investigate the star system ahead of us.

That decision falls to me.

I've never received more than the most cursory instructions in making such a determination; the ship's intelligence normally takes care of such matters.

Within moments, I decide. *Shovach* must have detected something in this system that caused it to awaken me. I could never forgive myself if we passed up this system when it might receive our species in a four-armed embrace.

———

The ship approaches this latest system from above the plane of its ecliptic, providing me with a broad view of its status. Though my mission does not find it strictly necessary, I prefer to examine a system as a whole before I focus on the three possible colony worlds here.

So: peering down at this system from this vantage point, I find that at its extreme edges lie a typical cometary cloud and lesser planets. Closer in, I can see a series of four gas giants. The farthest one out, Planet Eight, possesses beautiful deep blue surface clouds, a narrow ring, and several small moons.

The next planet in reveals another brace of moons, and clouds of a lighter blue than the previous world, but just as beautiful, to my eyes. But the few sensors that still operate also reveal a possible long-ago catastrophe -- this planet's rotation tilts drastically, making it appear as if the world rolls along on one side as it orbits its primary, taking its many small moons along for the ride. This represents more than simply an interesting anomaly, given that I've arrived from a world destroyed by such a collision. How many such systems have endured such violent encounters? The explorer within me wishes to examine it more closely, but my mission must come first. Continuing my examination of these outer worlds, Planet Six has an atmosphere made up primarily of hydrogen and helium, with wide bands of yellow and brown across its surface. It also has a large complement of moons that will surely cross orbits with one another over time. Their combined mass is such that their destruction could eventually cause them to form an extensive ring system.

If the Ytani species can settle somewhere within this system and re-establish a working society, imagine the possibilities for exploration before us!

Still looking down upon this system, Planet Five, the last of the gas giants looking inward, masses more than twice as much as the system's other worlds combined. Its atmosphere is also primarily hydrogen and helium, creating broad bands of brown, red, orange, and white across its surface. Another large set of moons revolves around it, which possibly could also form an eventual ring system. Farther into the system, I detect an asteroid belt, whether the remnants of a planet somehow destroyed, or one that never formed, I cannot tell.

But I have a much more important mission, one which will find no resolution while peering at these outer worlds, no matter how interesting I may find them. The ship, in its judgement, felt this system held sufficient potential that it awakened me to decide whether to pause here.

Now my decision sees us using precious energies for braking, life-support, and gravity so that I may examine this system -- a decision that conceivably risks the entire population of the ship. I must also consider *Shovach*'s capabilities to repair and resupply itself -- how many more such stops can it make before it must cease traveling altogether, preserving its energies to keep its crew alive?

With a few simple commands, I move *Shovach* down from above the ecliptic toward the inner system for a closer look. Rocky worlds rather than gas giants dominate here. None of them measures over thirteen thousand kilometers in diameter, which I find odd. This system contains no rocky worlds of a size larger than these planets but smaller than the gas giants, which sets it off as different from most other systems we've encountered.

I reverse the order in which I examine these rocky worlds, beginning at the innermost and working outward. The proximity to its sun makes the closest planet unsuitable, a hellish place that would never allow intelligent life to live upon it unprotected. This leaves me free to consider planets Two, Three, and Four, each of which shows qualities which may provide a new home for my people.

I aim *Shovach* at Planet Two and gather as many sensor capabilities as I can to take a series of readings. Some yield positive results; others register as more problematic. This world has water on much of its surface, even oceans. That bodes well for this world as a possible new home for the Ytani, but other factors, such as the lack of evidence of life in those waters, work against that possibility, as does this world's slow rotation. That rotation also manifests itself counter-clockwise, suggesting some sort of cosmic collision in this world's past, just as Planet Seven suffered.

I wish Rynon could help me interpret these readings in more detail, but I can't rationalize waking her just yet. That would place the same strain upon her body as it does mine, and I do not know how many awakenings she has left. Her life remains precious to me, perhaps more than my own, and I would not risk it lightly.

A world reveals itself in more ways than merely cataloging its attributes. Gravity, overall temperature, the nature of its atmosphere, the makeup of its crust and its core, will interact in ways that we find difficult to assess from orbit. Should I look upon a person I've just become aware of from a distance, taking in only the color of their crest and the gestures of their lower arms? No, I should speak with them, attempt to engage more of both their intellect and emotions, to gain a fuller sense of their nature.

That truth applies to this world, as well. Visual observation, sensor readings, and the movements of its oceans and tectonic plates only tell part of its story. To fully understand a world, I must travel down to its surface, watch and listen and understand.

———

That desire for knowledge leads me down to the *Shovach's* transport bay. As I enter, the ship indicates a particular transport craft for me to take down to the surface of Planet Two. Its advanced systems allow a single person to operate it in relative safety.

I pass a lower hand across the transport's controls, and the craft leaves the *Shovach*. I indulge myself in a brief fly-around the starship. First I examine the four bundled crew modules at its front, the only part of the ship I've known first-hand. They house the primary control room, the stasis chambers, the transport bay and engineering systems, and the crew quarters, which mostly go unused, since all but one or two of us remain asleep during most of our journey.

Behind the crew module lies many more four-bundles of modules vital to our eventual colonization effort, containing everything from power generators, earth-movers, water extraction devices, and countless other pieces of equipment needed to establish a colony on a foreign world. Together the crew and equipment modules make up about a third of *Shovach*'s length.

The rest of its eleven-kilometer length consists of our most precious cargo -- all those potential people, billions of them. Once I or one of the other adults who work as exploration specialists identify and recommend a potentially suitable world for colonization, we would awaken our ship's captain, Nalt. If Captain Nalt agrees with our recommendation, he would awaken several other adults for further consultation. If we reach a consensus, we would prepare for colonization.

Most of the eleven thousand of us would devote ourselves to establishing that basic colony upon the new world, with the rest of us remaining aboard *Shovach* maintaining our starship's systems and preparing the fertilized eggs for development as soon as we establish a colony.

Our greatest danger lies here; we must make sure we have picked the proper world, one that will allow our adults to survive and even thrive. And our colony must survive long enough for a new generation to take the places of the original adults. It means our future hangs on a knife's edge, with the real possibility that even after centuries of travel among dozens of star systems, we may yet perish as a species. Much depends upon the *Shovach*. Even though it can refuel and resupply itself using natural resources within a particular star system, the ship itself has a limited lifespan.

I fear not just for my own life and those still unborn aboard the *Shovach*. I also fear for the death of our heritage, our culture. Our scientific advances allowed us to escape the cataclysm that destroyed Ytani. Our political advances allowed nations that once made war against one another to join together and build the *Shovach*. The giant ship also contains copies of our most beloved and important artistic endeavors -- among them Gaveron's sculpture Four Hands of Freedom, the complete mind-songs of Engari, and the greatest dramatic and comedic performances by countless actors, our most difficult cultural profession.

It also features billions of images of the planet Ytani, including such natural wonders as the Spires of Salt, the Forests of Stone, and the Prismatic Ocean.

After that brief tour, I send the transport arcing downward toward this new world. As I draw nearer, I decide to land near the shoreline of one of its oceans. The relationship between a world's land masses and its seas defines much of its essential nature. I hope to discover whether this world currently contains life and whether it could sustain the remnants of my people.

Thick clouds obscure much of Planet Two's surface, but I can still make out many of its land areas. Long mountain ranges line some areas, others feature vast desert reaches, and several have wide rivers traversing them, but everywhere its surface colors lean toward brown and red, without the blues or greens of vegetation. Crossing over to an oceanic area, it looks as if few winds disturb the water's surface. Despite the presence of clouds over much of this world, I wonder whether significant storms ever whip up here, whether hurricanes ever lash its shores.

I guide the transport over a broad range of mountains and bring it down onto a wide and flat beach, well away from the ocean's edge. This world has no moon, therefore only its sun causes tides here, and they remain small.

I prepare to exit the transport. My colleagues have scoffed at me for making such forays, but I cannot rule out a world that possesses any potential until I set foot upon it. I hesitate to call this a technique. Perhaps I should only refer to it as a habit. And I admit it has not yielded a suitable world just yet. But I have ruled out worlds which I might have deemed suitable viewing them only from orbit, and avoided wasting time and resources.

It takes only moments for me to put on my groundsuit, which will provide me with sufficient oxygen and protect me from extremes of temperature, radiation, and pressure, and also prevent me from contaminating my surroundings. Sensor readouts, which I control with my lower arms, appear on the top and bottom of my helmet's faceplate. A transparent strip across the top of my helmet reveals the colors of my crest, even though no one exists here to see the nature of my emotions. A thin exoskeleton augments the strength of my upper arms. Thin but durable gloves allow me to retain much of the sensitivity of the hands and fingers of my lower arms.

I step out onto the planet's surface, the dirt beneath my boots yielding slightly. My first steps leave well-defined footprints. I understand other explorers often compose a "meaningful" statement as the first words spoken on a particular world, but I've never bothered with such frivolities, especially with no one around to hear them.

I stand on a slight rise, looking out toward the ocean's still waters. Thick clouds glide across gray skies. I wish I could open my helmet and smell the air, feel the soft breeze. I close my lower right hand into a fist and sensors confirm what I perceived from orbit, that the atmosphere consists mostly of carbon dioxide and a bit of oxygen -- not a mixture I could breathe. I would find the temperature, though, that of a cool day back home.

The home long ago turned to slag.

I make my way down to the sea. Its waters reflect the gray, overcast skies. Shallow waves embrace the sandy shore, reflecting the shallow nature of the oceans in general. This world contains no vast ocean depths where life often develops. Another fist, and my readings reveal no evidence of life in these waters, confirming for this specific area the more general readings I'd taken from orbit.

Yet this word has much potential. Protocols require me to consider how a world will evolve over many years, even centuries. If I find that this planet will soon enough become one which can support Ytani life, I can awaken Captain Nalt and recommend that we wait here.

I glance toward the sheath of clouds hiding the sun, which glows with a muted yellow light. From my observations in orbit, the length of its day amounts to just under 117 days, slower than any other planet in the system. Could we choose to live on such a world, that has a daylight period of 58 days?

Imagine living so many days in a row in perpetual sunlight, then the same number of days in darkness. Workers would have to deal with disrupted sleep patterns, our crops may require genetic engineering to grow at all, and temperature extremes may prove difficult to endure.

I don't possess enough information to assess Planet Two properly. I can't decide how to interpret the facts I do possess.

My dominant heart begins to race, with the secondary one following an instant later. I imagine my crest glows a bright gray with happiness.

Finally I have a reason to awaken Rynon.

———

I stand apart from Rynon's stasis chamber as it begins the process of awakening her. I watch as her eyes flutter open, and her delicate lower hands begin to move. I listen as the ship asks her the usual questions about her name, her function, and why the ship (at my urging) has awakened her.

The top of her stasis chamber opens, and Rynon sees me. I start toward her but as her crest turns a deep, angry red, I stop. "You decided to awaken me," she says. "Not the ship."

I lace the fingers of my lower hands and fold my upper arms. "I did."

Rynon swings her legs out of the chamber. "I suppose only I have the expertise to help you," she says, as her crest fades toward the yellow of suspicion.

"I believe you do," I told Rynon.

She tries to stand, her legs nearly give way, but she waves off my assistance. "Do you realize how many times I've awakened?"

"I . . . never checked."

"You should have. I've awakened twenty times. Each time takes more out of me."

"I must apologize," I tell Rynon. "I never knew."

Rynon's normally red eyes appear faded. Her outer eye sheaths hang low, perhaps partially obscuring her vision.

I explain about many of *Shovach*'s systems having gone

down, then keep my remarks focused on the mission: "Three planets exist in this system which could become candidates for colonization. I've already visited one of these worlds. It has much potential. An atmosphere that could evolve into one we could breathe. Oceans covering much of its surface."

"Enough potential, I assume, to waste one of my awakenings?"

"I don't consider it a waste," I say. "I need your help."

Rynon starts toward the crew quarters module. She pauses and looks back at my crest, which I realize must shine with the pink of nervousness and uncertainty. She says. "I already have doubts about this system. But I will examine it with you."

I feel only relief as she continues toward her quarters.

———

Within the hour, Rynon comes into the control room from her quarters. Her crest glows at the edge of suspicious yellow and the white of sadness. She moves slowly, and her eyes appear dimmer than their usual red hue. I ask her, "Did you have something to eat? Can I offer you anything?"

"We should examine your planet. The reason you awoke me."

"I'll prepare the transport."

"No. I want to look at it from here in orbit, first."

My crest surely glows red. "I've already performed as many of the sensor sweeps as I can from up here given *Shovach*'s limitations. Going back down to the planet would -- "

"Would waste our time even further. Show me the information you've already gathered."

I do so, everything from the slowness of the planet's rotation to the shallowness of its oceans to the layout of its mountain ranges. Also its mean temperatures and atmospheric composition and many other factors.

When I finish, Rynon goes over to the primary sensor station without a word. She sits and works, the sensitive fingers of her lower hands quickly gathering more information. I set aside my resentment and stand behind her. I cannot tell at first what goal she wishes to achieve with the readings she takes. Finally I ask: "What causes your interest in the planet's plate tectonics?"

Rynon turns to address me. "Looking at the composition of the atmosphere, the amount of surface water, and its distance from the sun, I can safely predict that Planet Two will grow much warmer over time."

"I hope," I say, "that such warming brings conditions more suited to life."

"It will advance far past such conditions. The water in the seas will eventually evaporate. And right now, the movement of this planet's tectonic plates depends upon the water which seeps into its mantle and lubricates such motion. Plate tectonics will end. Lava will flow across the planet's surface."

"So -- a catastrophe. One we cannot prevent."

The sight of Rynon's crest turning black, indicating genuine empathy for me, takes a bit of the sting from her words. "One catastrophe upon another. Without water, carbon dioxide will build up in the atmosphere. Planet Two will see a runaway greenhouse effect, as we've found on other worlds."

I say, "We have two other chances in this system to find a suitable planet for colonization."

Rynon says, "I have severe doubts."

"I feel more optimistic."

Rynon's crest fades from black to gray out of amusement toward me. "I suppose you feel -- what do you call it? -- that 'sense of wonder' you often exhibit at such times."

"I cannot deny that. To stand upon such a world, to imagine recreating the society we had -- "

"A dream, Draiora. Nothing more. But I will help you explore these other two worlds. Otherwise I have wasted an awakening."

My hearts soar at the thought of spending more time with Rynon, but I turn away from her so she won't see my crest glowing with the bright orange of joy and affection, completely inappropriate for our relationship as mere colleagues. Rynon heads toward her quarters, leaving me to guide the ship toward the next world in this system, Planet Three, which currently orbits on the same side of the sun as Planet Two.

———

Days later, the *Shovach* arrives at Planet Three, and Rynon joins me in the control room. She appears tired, I detect a slight limp in her left leg, and I almost ask her how she feels. I hold off, believing I worry too much. Hoping. We receive the good news, however, that *Shovach*'s healing protocols have yielded some success, especially when it comes to its sensor arrays. Together, Rynon and I perform a full range of sensor scans, hoping this world could become the new home for our species.

As we receive the first results from this world, though, I see that its surface roils in chaos, with volcanic eruptions across much of its rocky and barren landscape. Because of those eruptions, it possesses a carbon dioxide atmosphere and no oxygen. Comet strikes have provided enough water for oceans, which have become much deeper than those on the previous world. I even spot a tsunami nearing the coast of one conti- nent, no doubt engendered by one of the many earthquakes that transform its surface constantly. I find myself eager to examine Planet Three's wave patterns, given that unlike Planet Two, this one features a moon uncommonly large in relation to the world it accompanies.

I see Rynon glancing at my crest, which glows increasingly white as my disappointment with these results grows. "Go ahead," I tell her. "I know what you want to tell me."

Rynon's own crest shines unexpectedly blue with curiosity. "How can you know that?" She calls up a hologram of read-outs of a series of deep-ocean hot springs near the planet's equator. "Have you seen these results? The possibility of lifeforms?"

I peer at the hologram. My upper hands squeeze together in surprise, while my lower right points at the image. "In such an environment?"

"Yes, if fed by carbon dioxide, nitrogen, and hydrogen gases. As we see down there."

"I -- I have no further words in this moment. You show more optimism about this world than I can muster."

"A tentative optimism," Rynon says. "I assume you would like to examine this world up close?"

My breathing quickens. She doesn't usually care for making planetary landings. "Of course I would," I tell her.

Rynon starts toward the transport bay. "Then let us begin."

———

Rynon suggests that I pilot the transport down to Planet Three. As we draw nearer to this new world, I gain a closer look at details I previously saw only from orbit. The planet's nightside glows with the light of hundreds of volcanoes, with rivers of lava connecting many of them together. As we come around to the dayside, I have a better look at the oceans, which range over a much broader expanse of this world's surface than Planet Two's, and which sensors tell us descend far more deeply beneath its waves. I launch a probe which will search for one of the deep-water hot springs where Rynon's sensor search detected life. I consider this a slender hope, but my consciousness grasps it tightly.

"I'd like to land near an ocean," I tell Rynon. "But close enough to catch a view of a volcano."

"I approve of any choice you make," Rynon replies.

I can't help but glance over at her crest, which shines primarily blue with curiosity, but with some shadings of pink, indicating fear or nervousness. "Don't worry," I tell her, "I've done this plenty of times before."

Rynon's crest edges over into shades of red anger along with pink and blue. "I've done this many times, as well. But not with someone else piloting."

"But my piloting skills -- "

"I don't mean you, specifically. I mean I prefer controlling the transport myself."

"You could've asked to pilot."

Rynon says, "I apologize. My anger aims itself toward my own judgement, not toward your piloting skill."

I say no more until I land the transport upon a suitable, and relatively safe, plain, with an ocean a few hundred meters to the east and a large volcano about five kilometers to the west. The volcano's current lava streams flow in directions well away from our position, but the output of previous flows has hardened beneath the transport's skids.

Rynon and I put on our groundsuits. She takes her time, whether out of caution or fatigue, I can't tell. At the airlock, I tell her, "You can make the first step upon this world, if you wish."

Her crest, already a nervous pink, adds a yellow tint of impatience. "Do you consider that some sort of honor?"

"I find it exhilarating."

Rynon stands back from the door. "Then I gladly cede that honor to you."

I never sought this confrontation, however minor. Rather than continue it, I exit the transport first, Rynon following close behind.

My first footsteps on Planet Three fall onto quite a different surface than upon Planet Two. The ground doesn't give way to my boots. This type of lava flow eventually forms mountains.

I look toward the west, and the volcano standing near the horizon. Bright red lava erupts in a constant burst from its peak, and flows at a measured pace down its sides. Black clouds of ash and gases billow nearly straight up at a distance equalling its height before winds push them into a sharp turn to the northeast.

Rynon aims her portable sensor toward the volcano nearest us. "This one appears to have developed in a typical manner. It adds much carbon dioxide to the atmosphere, as all the others do."

"A drawback, of course," I say. "But it also brings the mean temperature above freezing across much of the planet. Otherwise this might have become an ice world."

Rynon lowers her portable sensor. "This world will never become inhabitable for us. This chaotic surface, the constant flow of deadly gases into the atmosphere -- "

The ground shifts and rumbles beneath our feet. My legs stiffen to remain standing, and my nerves continue to react to that movement and the low-pitched sounds of the earth for long seconds after they fade.

Rynon's crest shines with the unadulterated pinkish shades of fear. "That represents another reason we cannot inhabit this world."

"You showed more optimism before we left the ship."

"Perhaps you've shown me that your technique of coming down to a planet, to experience such a complex system from a vantage point on the surface, has some merit."

I turn away from Rynon and walk up a gradual rise overlooking the ocean. I look down upon massive waves striking a rugged shoreline, creating a constant roar. This ocean writhes as if in pain. From behind me I hear Rynon: "No ship could ever navigate such seas."

I look up at this world's moon, which fills more of the sky than any other natural satellite I've seen. I can make out erupting volcanoes on its surface, as well. "You could almost describe this as a double-planet system," I tell Rynon, "with both of them still in the process of forming themselves."

"Such a configuration might remain inherently unstable," Rynon says.

I ask, "What about the life in those hot springs?"

"Potential life. We'll wait for the probe to return."

I walk toward the transport. "Then let's wait back on *Shovach*."

———

Hours later, back aboard *Shovach* in the control room, Rynon and I examine the sensor results and images from the hot springs at the ocean's floor.

Rynon's crest glows with a combination of a dark blue of curiosity and a light brown of depression. "These beings survive on substances poisonous to us," she says.

The images from these ocean depths amaze me. Carbonate structures nearly thirty meters tall reach from the ocean's floor like fingers stretching toward an unseen goal. Hydrothermal vents blast gases made up of two parts hydrogen and one part sulfur into an environment where the water pressure stands at five hundred times that of sea level. And here lies life, and even a primitive ecosystem! Yet this discovery fails to console me.

"What advanced sort of life," I ask Rynon, "could possibly arise from such an ecology?"

"None that we would recognize, "Rynon says. And given the dominance of volcanoes on this world, it may never have the chance to develop on land at all."

"Even if it does -- you understand my fear."

"Yes, of course. If this kind of life develops and eventually dominates this world -- "

"It will not prove suitable for our kind of life, requiring oxygen and cooler temperatures to survive. Even if we wait many millennia. But will *Shovach* even have a chance to survive that long?"

Rynon's crest fades to a sad white. "If only we could find a world already suitable for us. Even one with intelligent beings already living upon it. We could ask for their assistance, or at least their mercy."

"We don't know how such things work. What if our species has gained intelligence before any other in the galaxy? We have to assume we'll receive no assistance from other intelligences."

Rynon says, "I wish things had turned out otherwise."

I reach toward the controls to send the *Shovach* toward the system's Planet Four. "We have one more world to examine," I say. "Let's hope Planet Four favors us more than the others."

"I agree," Rynon says. I worry about her as she heads for her quarters with a limp even more pronounced than before.

––––––

Within days, Rynon and I take the transport down to the surface of Planet Four. Rynon, who has insisted upon piloting herself this time, appears more energetic today, which heartens me. She shows great enthusiasm as I launch a series of drones on our way down to the surface. Those drones will take samples from various places on the land, both on the surface and underground, as well as deep within the oceans.

Rynon doesn't choose a site next to an ocean as I usually do. Instead, we land upon a high plateau overlooking a range of mountains, several rivers, and a lake 150 kilometers wide apparently formed long ago by a meteorite strike. Rynon's crest glows blue with curiosity. "I must admit I've come to admire your idea of examining a planet in person," she says. "Especially one with an oxygen atmosphere! I believe this lake may contain our best chance to discover life here, however primitive."

That promise excites me, as well. I can barely wait to put on my groundsuit. I hope Rynon doesn't notice that I take along a sample pack to investigate personally for signs of life.

"Please," Rynon tells me as we enter the airlock, "become the first person to set foot on this world, as well." I don't argue with her; instead, I cycle through the airlock, reminding myself of how carefully I'll have to move in this world's gravity, much lower than that of Planet Three. I rush away from the transport to take in as much of this world's beauty as I can, as quickly as I can.

White clouds cruise through blue skies, alternately shielding and revealing the morning sun. A line of low mountains stretches toward the horizon, fading into the distance. Several broad freshwater streams wind their way among the mountains they've carved out across millennia, while also feeding into that large lake. A mountain at the lake's center, which we can make out on the horizon, barely rises above its waters.

The nearer moon, much smaller and with an irregular shape compared to the giant moon of Planet Three, has already risen -- and in the west, because it orbits faster than this world rotates. Its rapid orbit will see it set in the east only to rise again in only eleven hours. I expect to see Planet Four's other moon, much smaller and farther away, rising in the east soon, as seems proper. Even smaller than the other moon, it will appear only as a small star in the night sky, though it will remain there for nearly three days.

We stand near Planet Four's equator. Water covers about a third of its surface, mostly in the northern hemisphere. I tell Rynon, "I feel this planet could easily support life. I hope we hear positive development from our drones." Their findings would complement those of the sensor sweeps from *Shovach*.

"I must admit," Rynon says, "that this world may represent the best opportunity for us to find a new homeworld." She consults her portable sensor. "Such an oxygen-rich atmosphere may show us the way. And so much fresh water!"

"And so beautiful! Imagine what secrets lie within those hills and mountains, beneath those waters! I wish I could just open my helmet and take a deep breath, take fresh air deeply into all my lungs and smell the true nature of this planet. To really know this world, to understand it on such a visceral level!"

Rynon's crest turns pink with concern. "You can't do that! It has an oxygen-rich atmosphere, yes, but not enough for us to survive. And we don't know whether it contains microbes that could harm us."

"Don't worry. The idea tempts me, but not enough to actually do it."

"You mean, not enough for me to have to carry your body back into the transport."

I say, "If we find life here, we'll have to come back down after we wake up more of the crew. And we should bring surface transport, and housing, and -- "

Rynon says, "Don't use four arms where two will do. We need more information from our drones." One of her sensors beeps. "Such as the information coming in right now."

Rynon looks at the sensor readout. Even as I watch, her crest turns a deep gray, indicating her happiness. "What do you see?" I ask.

"Possible signs of life all over this planet. In caves, in hydrothermal vents such as we saw on Planet Three. And -- " She indicated the giant lake before us. "Right in there."

I look across this landscape once more. I stare down the slope right in front of me toward the large lake, the closest body of water to us, its still waters a bright blue reflecting the skies. I tell Rynon, "I want to go down to that lake and take some direct readings."

Rynon's crest fades toward pink. "Don't make such a dangerous move," she says. "We haven't had that much experience with exploration on a planetary surface."

I lean over to check out the slope again -- I estimate it amounts to about a thirty meter trip. "I just have to take care going down this hill. It doesn't look very steep or rough. The lighter gravity here will make it easier, as well."

Rynon's pink crest edges toward red anger. "I will not come after you if you fall."

I don't mention that I believe she would. Besides, I don't intend to fall. "Don't worry about me," I say as I take the first tentative step down the hill.

Rocky and uneven ground makes for slower progress than I'd anticipated. About halfway down, I look back. Rynon hasn't spoken, I assume to avoid distracting me. I can barely see her crest glowing with a combination of pink concern and yellow impatience.

I reach the edge of the lake. Thankfully, neither moon exerts enough gravitational force to create tides, and what little breeze sweeps across this area only ripples the lake's waters, barely moistening the rocks at its edge. I kneel down and extend a small arm on my sample pack to scoop up a small sample of water.

Now Rynon speaks. "What did you just do?"

"I gathered a couple of small samples. No more."

The briefest of pauses. "Samples which will have to undergo decontamination even before we lift the transport off this planet."

I activate the sensors within the sample packs. "I don't intend to take them back. We have no reason to bring samples aboard the ship if they don't indicate lifesigns. If we do find lifesigns, we'll want to bring more extensive testing facilities down here."

I look at the initial results from the sample packs. For a moment, I can't speak. Finally Rynon asks, "Draiora, you have the grayest looking crest I've ever seen. What have you found?"

I force myself to speak. "Only -- life."

Since I can't see Rynon's crest, I infer her emotions from her hesitant, yet eager vocal qualities. "What kind of life?"

"Bacteria. They look like chemolithoautotrophs, living on carbon dioxide either in the water or the air."

Rynon said, "That looks promising. Perhaps we should wake up some of the others and have them examine this evidence."

"We'll have more information once we return to the ship and look at the results from the rest of our probes."

I leave the water sample where it lies and start back up the rocky hill, paying no attention to the exertion involved, eager to return to *Shovach*. I wonder whether I've discovered the world that could become the new home for our species.

———

After Rynon and I arrive back aboard the *Shovach*, we go immediately to the control room. Each of us calls up more information from our many drones -- holos, flat images, and displays of countless numbers showing us details of this world's composition, atmosphere -- and possible life.

I point a lower arm at one readout detailing the nature of that life. "I can barely believe what this tells us," I tell Rynon. "It seems life fills this world wherever we see water."

Rynon steps closer to that display, and her crest reveals both gray happiness and pink uncertainty. "You seem concerned," I say.

Rynon waves away several displays and brings up others. "We still haven't found a suitable world."

I struggle to hold my emotions in check as I ask, "What problem have you found?"

Rynon indicates a series of readouts. "Actually I've found two problems. Between Planet Four's low gravity letting the atmosphere seep away, and the solar wind stripping much of it away, it will lose the ability to sustain life."

I look away from the displays, wishing I could hide my crest, which glows with the bright white of sadness and grief. "How soon would this happen?"

Rynon looks back toward the displays. "Not for many centuries, of course."

"But any colony we established in those centuries would die out. I must apologize, Rynon. I've wasted one of your awakenings."

"And also your own, Draiora. I appreciate your own sacrifice."

"I don't care about that. I can make such a decision for myself. But I can't forgive myself for making the wrong decision for you. Each person who awakens has the path of their life chipped away little by little, until nothing remains."

"We should've passed this system by, "Rynon says. "But I can't blame you for that. You didn't have the experience. I expect now, though, that you've learned quite a bit from exploring these three worlds."

"Much of this world reminds me of our homeworld. Perhaps that motivated me to see the possibilities here. These mountains with so many rivers and lakes flowing among them remind me of a smaller version of the Thousand Mountain Range back on Ytani. I . . . suppose you'll return to stasis soon."

"I have no reason to remain awake."

Rynon doesn't mean for her words to do more than state a fact, but they still sting. Despite the frustration of failing to find a suitable world, I've cherished the time I've spent with my mentor. But I tell her, "I understand."

"Let's set the *Shovach*'s controls to take us out of this system," Rynon says. "Then we can speak some more."

As we program the ship to take us out of this star system, to continue its long search for a possible home for our people, we take one last look at Planet Four, which held such promise and hope in the flowing waters among its many mountain ranges, and in its bright blue skies.

Then Rynon says, "Come with me to the stasis chamber." she says. "We can talk as I prepare for my next sleep."

As we make our way there, I notice Rynon's limp has returned. Just as we enter the stasis chamber, the leg with the limp collapses and she stumbles and falls. I reach out with my upper arms and lower her to the floor as gently as I can. She tries but cannot move her own upper arms. Her lower arms reach out to me. "You have to carry me to my chamber."

"Shouldn't I try to get you to the infirmary?"

"It'll take too long to prepare itself to treat me. And you don't have medical training. The stasis chamber cannot heal me, but it can preserve me."

I use my upper arms to pick Rynon up from the floor, and my lower ones to steady her. As I carry her toward her stasis chamber I see that her crest glows a bright pink. Her fear triggers my own, and I carry her to her chamber and place her inside as gently as I can.

I help Rynon with the preparations for her next long sleep, hoping her next awakening will take place at a world where all the remaining Ytani species can live. She tells me, "As eager as I remain to help you, Draiora, you cannot awaken me again. Not unless we have arrived at a new home for our species, and our doctors know the treatment I will require the moment I awaken."

I cannot control the racing of my dominant heart. I tell Rynon, "I understand. If I find us a suitable world the next time I awaken . . . "

"Whether you make that discovery, or anyone else, Draiora, I hope to see you again." I close the stasis chamber's transparent cover. The mist of sleep fills the chamber and I watch as Rynon's eyes close and the pink cast of her crest fades.

The chamber fills with the liquid nutrients that will sustain her through the next years or centuries of sleep, and soon I can make out only the bare outline of her form.

I go to my own chamber and prepare it to accept me. Before I lay myself down within it, however, I make one change to the awakenings schedule. Rather than rotating resurrections among the other fifty-four individuals the ship could choose, I reprogram it always to awaken me. Each time, every time the ship detects a system that might contain a new planet for the Ytani.

As my chamber's cover closes, I see the pink uncertainty my crest reveals reflected within it.

I think of the ship's usual first question whenever I awaken. Yes, I know my name, Draiora.

I consider what that name means. It belongs to one of the last refugees from the doomed planet Ytani, someone eager to work, perhaps the rest of his often-interrupted life, to find a new home for his species.

That will take a toll, but even though years and centuries of repeated sleeps and awakenings have ravaged my body, others have fared much worse. I cannot let them, and I especially cannot let Rynon, sacrifice their health, their very lives, for me.

My body begins to cool. As I wait for the chamber to fill with liquid, I wonder whether any of these worlds, no matter how unsuitable as a homeworld for the Ytani, will ever develop intelligent life of their own. I wish I could return to this star system a few hundred thousand or even a billion years from now. I would feel sad, viewing the results of a runaway greenhouse effect that surely would have ravaged Planet Two by then. And I would grieve, seeing whether Planet Three's dominant life form, as I suspected, had indeed developed from beings in the deep ocean hot springs who live in an environment that would poison us.

But as consciousness fades, I allow myself the fantasy that Planet Four, so evocative of Ytani, with limitless water and skies of endless blue, could become a paradise, perhaps engendering an intelligent species that might, one day, rival my own.

AFTERWORD

"The Dominant Heart Begins to Race" is a story that began forming after I read an article about what the planet Mars might have been like four billion years ago. It seems it could've been pretty Earth-like. That had me wondering which planet in our Solar System an alien race back then would believe to be the most likely candidate for colonization. It certainly wouldn't be the Earth! And the idea that Mars would seem to be the most suited intrigued me.

I had to raise the stakes for the Ytani so this would be more than just a casual exploratory mission. Unfortunately, that meant I had to destroy their homeworld. This added urgency to Draiora's mission, and to tighten the screws on him even more, I added the complicated relationship with his mentor Rynon. When a story deals with "widescreen" issues such as the destruction of someone's homeworld and the possible extinction of their species, it's doubly important to bring the focus down to individual characters. Their reactions to the events of the narrative and the decisions they make become the story, which is as it should be.

After this story's original appearance in ANALOG, one reader pointed out that I'd referred to Saturn's rings, yet they probably hadn't formed four billion years ago. I decided in the story's appearance here to stick to current scientific knowledge and rewrote the scene. But I really loved Draiora catching sight of those rings!

Beyond Human Measure

I'd mentioned Jupiter whales in my earlier story "The Loophole," and I wanted to learn more about those beings. The story idea I came up with also allowed me to bring back one of my series characters, Carrie Molina, who had appeared in the stories "Stealing Adriana" and "Midwife Crisis." All of the above stories originally appeared in ANALOG SCIENCE FICTION magazine and were reprinted in my earlier collection, THE HUMAN EQUATIONS.

In this tale, Carrie not only has another unwanted encounter with the man who killed her sister, she must accompany him on an unlikely mission of mercy.

———

"It is when we try to grapple with another man's intimate need that we perceive how incomprehensible, wavering, and misty are the beings that share with us the sight of the stars and the warmth of the sun."

-- Joseph Conrad, Lord Jim

———

If Carrie Molina had ever anticipated making this trip past Jupiter's wispy ring into the gas giant's outer atmosphere, she'd never have guessed her attention wouldn't be focused upon the magnificence of the bank of cirrus clouds made of ammonia crystals stretching a thousand kilometers ahead of the shuttle. Or that she'd barely notice the distant sun, one-fifth its size as seen from Earth.

Or that her thoughts wouldn't be focused upon the all-important rescue mission, but upon the passenger sitting directly behind her.

Given Malcolm Vicari's presence, her primary thought was, *It seems crime isn't always punished — in this case, it may end up being rewarded.*

Vicari, the key to the rescue mission, was also the man who had abused and killed Carrie's sister three years earlier.

A wave of guilt passed through Carrie's consciousness — Vicari was here to save a peacemaker's life — and, in doing so, to save countless other lives as well.

"We're only about fifteen hundred K from the target," the pilot sitting to Carrie's right said as the sky faded from a star-filled black to a blue eerily reminiscent of Earth's. Carrie, who was serving as the shuttle's co-pilot, forced herself to return her attention to its controls. Kayonga Tedesco, tall, dark-skinned, and bald, had piloted this shuttle, the *Elaine Shackleton*, on such journeys nearly a dozen times, making him the best bet to guide it toward their destination, hundreds of kilometers into Jupiter's atmosphere.

Carrie and Vicari had just arrived from Earth to be part of this hastily-organized mission.

The shuttle dove into the dark realms of hydrogen and helium clouds; a forked bolt of lightning large enough to have blasted Chicago or Atlanta from the face of the Earth stabbed downward to their right.

"Just over a thousand K from the target," Kayonga said. Carrie kept a close eye on the instruments; the view out the forward screen showed mostly darkness. Thanks to the shuttle's inertials, they couldn't feel the buffeting of the 600-kph winds against the craft.

Vicari pushed back several strands of his shoulder-length black hair as he spoke for the first time since leaving Callisto Base: "I've never made such a long trip just to make a new friend."

Carrie couldn't help tensing up at the sound of his voice; memories of the empty shell that was her sister's body arrived unbidden. She turned toward him and muttered, as much to herself as to him, "Shut the hell up."

"Why, Carrie, you should be nicer to the person who will be our friend's savior."

Kayonga tapped the console in front of Carrie and she turned back around. "Sorry," she told him.

But Kayonga's gaze didn't stray from the controls and readouts as he told Vicari, "You heard the woman. Shut the hell up."

"Oh, a consensus," Vicari said. "Let's see your opinion of me once we make contact with Lykohnel."

"Don't worry," Carrie told Kayonga. "I can ignore him."

"Let's do," Kayonga said. "About two hundred K from target."

"The winds have died down a bit."

"Yeah, I see — 'only' about 450 kph now. Should make final approach easier, though."

Soon, despite interference from Jupiter's own magnetic field, sensor bounceback combined with heat signatures provided a picture of the "target" — a "Jupiter whale" named

Lykohnel, a cylindrical being half a kilometer long and over a hundred meters wide. She was what scientists referred to generally as a "floater," the interior of her body filled with helium and heavier gases, allowing her to glide safely along as she lumbered within the depths of Jupiter's atmosphere. In one moment, Lykohnel might cruise along the top of a 500-K wide storm system like a surfer riding a wave. The next moment her ponderous body might turn to one side to propel herself more efficiently against a crosswind.

The Human term "whales" was an early misnomer that stuck; they resembled whales not so much as dirigibles, and typically traveled in groups of a hundred or more.

Vicari said, "She's beautiful."

Carrie's first instinct was to tell him again to shut up, but she couldn't deny his statement. *She is beautiful,* she thought. *All her movements take place as if in slow motion, but they're deliberate and calculated.*

Humanity had no idea how many Jupiter whales existed — estimates ranged from tens of thousands to hundreds of millions. Certainly, Jupiter's immense size, over eleven times the diameter of Earth, provided plenty of room for such beings. The shuttle's long-range sensors were largely useless here, given the strength of Jupiter's magnetic fields and its turbulent atmosphere, but Carrie knew two groups of whales, each thousands strong, were waiting several thousands of kilometers away, one to the east of Lykohnel's position, the other to the west.

"Let's see if she can hear us," Kayonga said, and opened a comm channel. "This is Kayonga Tedesco. Lykohnel — I've returned, with new friends this time."

A burst of static came back over the comm, but quickly resolved into a clear and confident voice: "I welcome Kayonga. I am glad you have returned."

"How are you feeling, my friend? I hope you are recovering from your injuries."

Lykohnel's voice seemed less certain of itself now: "It has been . . . a difficult process."

Vicari leaned forward between Carrie and Kayonga. "Ask her what I can do. What are the extent of her injuries — is she is pain? How can — "

Carrie told him, "Shut the hell up!"

Kayonga placed a hand on her arm. Carrie couldn't help seeing that he only now noticed her webbed fingers. They'd met only minutes before this emergency run. "Easy," Kayonga said. "Those are legitimate questions." He turned his attention to Vicari. "We've got to go slowly, though. The whales' thought processes are . . . leisurely. Or maybe I should say methodical. It doesn't indicate a lack of intelligence — just that they're very large beings who don't move quickly, and don't act rashly."

Vicari gave a mock salute. "Understood. I'll just sit back here for now."

See that you do, Carrie thought. She asked Kayonga, "This is going to be similar to a rendezvous and docking, isn't it?"

"That's right," Kayonga said. "I've actually found it's best to hover over Lykohnel's back and let her come to the shuttle. Once we set down, we can start working."

Vicari said, "You mean I can start working."

Carrie said, "Listen, be glad you've been given the freedom to come out here at all. Once you cure Lykohnel, it's back to prison for you."

Kayonga asked, "Not rehab?"

"I've always refused it," Vicari said.

Carrie kept her eyes on the image of Lykohnel, which was becoming more detailed even in visible light. She said, "He loves himself too much."

"Not at all, my dear. I'm simply too much in love with knowledge. I fear that undergoing mental rehabilitation to eliminate what you consider to be my 'disorder' would also eliminate my curiosity — I will not stand for that."

Vicari, using nanotech he'd created and implanted within his body, had given himself the ability with only a touch to send electrical charges through a person's limbic system, which modulates emotional responses, memory, and other functions.

It amounted to a neural attack, in which he could evoke a particular emotion in his victim — fear, sexual desire, whatever he wished. Those emotions were also seared into his own memory, and he could relive them whenever he wished.

He'd used that ability to abuse several women, including Carrie's sister Adriana. She'd been left essentially brain-dead, all her emotions and self-awareness stripped from her body. Soon even that body died.

Carrie, a "fixer" for the Earth Unity, had captured Vicari within an orbital habitat and taken him down to the Earth. Vicari, tried and sentenced for his crimes, and having refused mental rehab, remained one of the few convicted criminals on Earth detained within a prison.

Kayonga said, "We're coming up on Lykohnel. We're going to hover about thirty meters directly over her."

"Understood," Carrie said.

"Lykohnel — we're ready."

"I am adapting my colors as I approach," the Jupiter whale said. Her body could change colors from black to blue to orange to yellow as needed for camouflage. In this instance, she changed her color to a bright yellow so it could best be seen against the swirling clouds of Jupiter's atmosphere.

Carrie watched, fascinated, as Lykohnel's immense body rose steadily toward the shuttle. When she drew to within about ten meters, she slowed until her ascent was barely perceptible. Carrie hardly felt the moment of actual contact.

"Very good," Kayonga said. "Deploying contact module."

Vicari asked, "What does that mean?"

Carrie fought to hold back her emotions as she told him, "The module extends down from the outer airlock hatch to Lykohnel's skin. It'll maintain life support so we don't have to worry about lifesuits."

Vicari said, "I see. So I can touch our friend directly."

"Directly — and properly," Carrie said. "My eyes will be on you every moment."

Lykohnel had been injured in a physical altercation while trying to mediate between two groups of whales who claimed the same feeding areas. The whales fed upon much smaller lifeforms that swarmed deep within Jupiter's atmosphere. They had to descend deep enough into its clouds that they risked being crushed by the pressure — that was also a time they were vulnerable from attacks by other whales.

The whole conflict seemed ridiculous to Carrie; the disputed area was the size of several Earths, with plenty of room for all. But Lykohnel's first attempt at negotiations had failed after violence broke out among the two sides. Leaders of both factions, however, were now willing to begin talks again, but only with Lykohnel. Everything depended upon Vicari healing Lykohnel.

"Module's in place," Kayonga said. "Safe environment confirmed. Let's go." He opened the shuttle's inner airlock hatch, then the outer one, and led the way though them both. Carrie grabbed a sensorpac, but held back and let Vicari go ahead of her.

"Don't trust me?" Vicari asked.

"Not enough to turn my back on you."

"You're welcome," Vicari said, and followed Kayonga onto

the surface of Lykohnel's back. The contact module was about six meters square, giving them plenty of room to work.

When Carrie set foot upon the whale's skin, she was surprised at how unyielding it was. *I expected to bounce back when I made that first step,* she thought. The yellow (for now) skin showed many pits and small tears — Carrie had no way of knowing whether the damage was from other whales who had attacked her or was just the normal battering any lifeform would take here in Jupiter's turbulent atmosphere.

Carrie asked Vicari, "So how does this work?"

Vicari replied, "If I understand correctly, the whales can actually store up electrical charges through an organ located here on their backs."

"That's right," Kayonga said. "It's how they communicate, using those charges at a low level."

"But at higher levels — ?"

"They can attack one another. That's what happened to Lykohnel."

Vicari looked at Carrie. "And that's where I come in. Her ability to store and direct those charges properly has been damaged, even the parts that regulate her bodily functions."

"You're talking just to hear yourself," Carrie said.

Vicari smiled as if he were a child just offered his favorite piece of chocolate. "But you'll keep listening anyway. If Lykohnel dies, we might see a civil war over those feeding areas. And how many other Jupiter whales will die then? Dozens — hundreds?"

Kayonga said, "We're listening. What do you need to do?"

"I have certain abilities — " Vicari began.

Which you used to strip my sister of her sanity and eventually kill her, Carrie thought.

" — and I can use those abilities to allow Lykohnel to

channel her electrical charges in the proper way. It's quite a fascinating proposition, actually."

Kayonga said, "I don't care how fascinating it is. Just help her. Lykohnel, are you ready for contact with this Human?"

Carrie heard Lykohnel's voice over her datalink: "I am ready."

Vicari said, "I'll walk all of you through this so it's clear what I'm doing." Vicari got down on one knee. "I'm going to touch the surface of her skin, here. Then it's just a matter of concentration. I can embrace her emotions, calm her, and assist in her healing." Vicari spread his hands wide and placed them on the surface of Lykohnel's skin. He closed his eyes and bowed his head.

After Vicari remained unmoving for several minutes, Kayonga motioned Carrie over to one corner of the module. He spoke in a low voice: "Is this guy for real? 'Embrace her emotions?'"

Carrie kept looking at Vicari as she told Kayonga, "He does have, as he said, 'certain abilities.' You know what he did to my sister."

"I do. And I share in your grief. I'll be praying for her tonight."

"Thank you," Carrie said. *I appreciate the gesture,* she thought. *But not being a believer, it's cold comfort to me.* She said, "As far as Vicari goes — in this instance I'm going to assume what he says is true."

"How can you trust him like that?"

"I never said I trusted him. There's only one thing he could do that would make me do that — die. That would definitely build my faith in the man's future actions -- or lack of them."

"You don't seem to have any illusions about him."

"Most kids had an imaginary friend. I had an imaginary enemy. It kept me alert."

"You don't have to kid like that for my sake, Carrie."

"I wasn't kidding." She raised the sensorpac. "Looks like he's made a good contact. And the electrical activity in Lykohnel's body is becoming more coherent."

Kayonga said, "Damn if he isn't doing it!" He looked toward Vicari. "I had severe doubts about this whole thing, and I don't mind admitting that."

"Whatever we might think about his morals — or lack of them — he's good at what he does." Images of Adriana's face in the lingering days before her death rose within Carrie's consciousness — her smooth face and vacant eyes, nothing left of the woman who always found a way to reach out with love and understanding in any situation.

A piercing scream, and Vicari fell backwards, all his limbs seizing, his head bouncing against the hard surface of Lykohnel's back. "The hell!" Carrie said, and ran toward Vicari, but before she could reach toward him, Kayonga told her, "Don't touch him!"

"But he's — "

"Trying to hold him down could hurt him more than his flailing about does. I'm going for a medkit." Kayonga bounded through the airlock into the shuttle.

Carrie stared down at Vicari, whose body continued its uncontrolled movements unabated. *Despite my first instinct being to come and help him,* she thought, *I actually have no problem with watching him flail around like that.*

I might actually come to enjoy it.

As Kayonga came back through the airlock, Vicari's seizure appeared to be subsiding. As Kayonga pulled a medical sensor from the kit, he asked, "Lykohnel — how are you? Were you harmed, as well?" Kayonga was making a quick scan on Vicari even as Lykohnel replied, "I was not harmed. Not anymore than I already was."

"Thank goodness for that," Carrie said.

Vicari's body went limp. Kayonga, continuing his scan, said, "Whatever happened, its effects are subsiding. Oh, crap!"

Carrie's heart raced, though her concern was for Lykohnel's prospect for treatment rather than Vicari. "What is it? Is he going to die?" *And if so, how long will it take me to come to terms with my feelings about that?*

Kayonga looked up from the medical scanner. "I don't know. But now his body's showing the same kind of damage Lykohnel's was. We have to get him back to Callisto Base."

———

It was the work of the better part of an hour to get Vicari back up to Callisto Station and into its infirmary. Another hour passed before Dr. Grace Vargas came out of the O.R. to tell Carrie and Kayonga, "He's still touch-and-go, but I'm hoping I can pull him through."

"What the hell happened to him?" Carrie asked.

"Some kind of feedback mechanism when he made contact with Lykohnel. We should've realized this wouldn't be easy — different species living in vastly different environments, and all that. Not the mention the difference in size between Jupiter whale and Human."

Kayonga asked, "Will he be able to make another try?"

Dr. Vargas's back stiffened. "If I have anything to say about it. But he's sustained some serious internal injuries."

Carrie pressed her lips together, but in spite of her best efforts, she found herself smiling, and suppressing a chuckle. Seeing Dr. Vargas's dismayed expression, she told her, "I'm sorry. I know you have to look kindly toward all your patients."

Dr. Vargas shook her head. "I know his history with you. Can't say as I blame you."

Kayonga asked, "When should we know something?"

Dr. Vargas rubbed her temples. "Within a day. How's Lykohnel doing?"

"Not well, last we heard," Carrie said. "So, as little sympathy as I have for Vicari, I have to hope you can make him well enough to treat her."

"I'll do my best," Dr. Vargas said.

We have to hope that's good enough, Carrie thought. As Dr. Vargas returned to her patient, she told Kayonga, "Let's go talk about what's next."

———

They went to the Callisto Station commissary, and soon Carrie was sipping on hot tea as Kayonga sat with a cup of coffee in front of him. "I'm gonna tell you flat out," Carrie said. "The instant Vicari was hurt, my secret hope was that he might never recover."

Kayonga glared at her. "That doesn't help Lykohnel any."

Carrie stared at her teacup. She drew in short breaths, and her head was pounding. "I didn't say I was proud of the thought. I hope you understand that as much as I'd like to see Vicari suffer, or even die, I'm even more eager to save Lykohnel."

"I'll be just as honest with you. I was surprised, given your history with him, that you were put on this mission."

"It's because of that background that I'm here. That, and my experience with another large aquatic creature on the planet Welkin. I helped deliver its baby — from the inside!"

Carrie savored watching Kayonga's expression open up as his mouth formed a wide grin. "You're kidding!"

"Not at all. I've had a pretty eventful few years. The Welkin thing on the upside. On the downside — Adriana, and my father dying during the Jenregar incursion back on Earth."

"I'm sorry. It's been a tough time for you, then."

"I had to leave the Earth. I did my share to fight the Jenregar. We won. I decided it's time to do something for myself, find a quiet little world, maybe something low-G, with some nice beaches, some nice tall glasses of liquor, and some nice tall men. Or short men, I don't really have a preference there."

"And instead you find yourself back with Vicari. What's he getting out of this?"

"Out of prison for awhile. It's an odd word even to say, isn't it? Most people agree to mental rehab."

"So he gets his little taste of freedom. And the entire time you get to relive one of the worst moments of your life."

Carrie's grasp tightened on her cup. "Doesn't seem like a fair trade, does it?"

Kayonga indicated Carrie's webbed hands. "I suppose you'd enjoy a swim at that nice beach even more than most of us."

Carrie smiled. Her body was bio-engineered to allow her to exist underwater for long periods without breathing equipment, and her webbed fingers and toes made swimming that much easier. "It does make a difference." Carrie felt her shoulders relax, her breathing grow calmer. "How long since you've been on a beach?"

"About five years ago, I guess. Right before I came out here. Beyin Beach in Ghana. One of my favorite spots. Sand soft and beautiful. Tall palms almost right up to the edge of the water. Fishermen and women hauling up their nets."

"Sometime when I'm back on Earth, I'll have to go there."

"I'd be more than happy to show you around. Though who knows when we'd both find ourselves back on Earth . . . "

Carrie took Kayonga's hand in hers. "I'd . . . love to get to know you better. But just . . . not for awhile."

Kayonga squeezed Carrie's hand. "I understand."

"Right now — I need to get something to eat. My mods give me a high metabolism. Then some sleep."

"We should know something by tomorrow morning, I hope."

"Yeah," Carrie said. "I just hate that I find myself rooting for the best for Vicari."

———

The next morning, Dr. Vargas met with Carrie and Kayonga in her office. As everyone seated themselves, the doctor said, "He's definitely going to live — for now."

"What does that mean — for now?"

"The nanotech that was letting him treat Lykohnel complicates things."

"How so?" Kayonga asked.

"His body's become dependent upon it to keep his own physiology running properly. His own immune system, limbic system, even just basic reflexes — they've all been degraded."

Carrie asked, "Which means?"

"Which means he's likely to die in the next few days. He's already paralyzed from the neck down. The only way he can even go back down to Lykohnel is to use an exoskeleton that also provides life support — that breathes for him, keeps his heart running, pretty much does about everything that keeps you alive."

"So, what is his nanotech doing?"

"Still giving him the ability to help Lykohnel, fortunately — if he has the chance."

Carrie managed to keep her voice steady as she said, "Which also means he keeps the ability to . . . . "

"Yes," Dr. Vargas said. "Do to anyone else the same thing he did to your sister, and his other victims."

Carrie could only nod. "That'll be great news for Lykohnel, at least if he lives long enough. But, the *bastard*."

Kayonga said, "Yes, but he's our bastard. We need him."

Carrie stood. "I want to talk to him."

"Do you think that's a good idea?"

"No," Carrie said. "But I want to do it anyway."

———

Carrie entered Vicari's cramped room in the station's infirmary. The man was lying still in his bed, apparently asleep. Sensors above the headboard and along the sides of the bed frame monitored his condition. From what little Carrie understood of their readouts, the man wasn't in good shape. The room had what Carrie thought of as that distinctive hospital smell.

Looking more closely at Vicari, even the skin over his face seemed to be sagging. His mouth stood open slightly, making him look pitiful. His chest rose and fell rhythmically in a manner that revealed the artificial origins of each breath.

"Vicari," Carrie said. He didn't respond. She raised her voice just a bit. "Vicari!"

Still nothing, at least for a few moments. But finally Vicari's eyes fluttered open. They widened at the sight of Carrie. His voice sounded strained: "I suppose if this were a bad cube drama I'd say this is when you came to gloat over my situation. But I know you're a better person than that."

Carrie said, "You might not know me as well as you think."

"Oh, I don't doubt you're gloating on the inside. You're not a saint."

"I *am* finding it hard to conjure up any sympathy for you. And you know, I'm OK with that."

"If I could move my hands, Carrie, I'd applaud you. Instead, I can only ask you what brought you here."

"I want to make sure you're going to try again to save Lykohnel."

"Of course I will. Why would I not?"

Carrie indicated Vicari's limp body. "Well, the first time didn't work out so well."

Vicari favored Carrie with a mock smile. "As I am well aware of. However, the doctors assure me that they'll have me up and around in an exoskeleton later today."

Carrie knew that she should thank Vicari, praise him for his commitment to the mission far beyond what anyone would be expected to do. But in the instant before she spoke, the familiar images of Adriana's unseeing eyes prevented her from speaking. She couldn't make herself look at Vicari for a moment — instead, she stared at the flashing lights and moving lines of the various medical readouts along his bed that were documenting the progress of what he had left of his life.

Vicari asked, "You're wondering why I'm doing this, aren't you?"

Carrie looked up at him with narrowed eyes. "You know I am."

Vicari said, "You know me primarily through my actions regarding your sister."

"You mean torturing her, recording her reactions to relive later, then leaving her to die."

Vicari continued: "I do what I must for my own good. If

others suffer, I find it regrettable, but I proceed anyway. As do we all."

"Not in the way you do."

"That's true, I suppose. But that suffering leads to greater insights for myself — into the nature of that suffering, into the feelings one has as they realize they are dying. It's difficult for someone like you to understand, I know."

Carrie wanted to leap onto the bed and throttle the man. "Is there a point here?"

"I am fascinated by these creatures — these Jupiter whales. As fascinated by them as I am by anything I've experienced with a Human."

Carrie felt tears welling up in her eyes, and kept them wide, not willing to give this man the satisfaction of seeing her cry.

Vicari continued: "Carrie, I wish you could've felt what I did in the moments before the feedback incident injured me. I felt Lykohnel's consciousness, and its immensity matches her physical size. She's what Humans call an 'old soul,' and her mind contains a wisdom Humanity has never dreamed of."

"What do you care about 'old souls,' or about Lykohnel's consciousness? You only care about — "

"About torture and death, I know. But you confuse the source of my feelings with what those feelings mean. I recall being four years old sitting in daycare and wishing for my mother's presence again — and the love that filled me at the first sight of her as she came into the room. I know of the transcendent physicality of the sex act. I know you're not a religionist, Carrie. Neither am I, because what loving God would create someone like me? But I've also read of the ecstasy Thomas Aquinas says he experienced in contemplating God."

"The point!" Carrie insisted, as, uncaring now, she let the tears fall.

Vicari smiled. "The point, my dear woman, is that of all those various feelings of Human ecstasy, those I've heard of, or those I've experienced myself, none of them compares with what I felt when I made contact with Lykohnel."

Carrie shook her head. "What do you want me to say?"

"I don't expect you to congratulate me on my good fortune. I just wanted to reassure you that I intend to carry out this mission. If I live long enough. I'm a selfish man. As I said earlier, I do what I must for my own good. And it's all to the good that I have that feeling again."

Carrie found her mouth forming a wan smile. "And then, even if you do last long enough to help Lykohnel, most likely you die."

Vicari closed his eyes for a moment, as if listening to a sound from far away. Then he said, "Yes. So we both get something we want, don't we?"

Carrie didn't feel the need to respond. She was more than happy to turn toward the doorway and leave Vicari all alone.

No sooner did she reach the corridor, though, than she found Kayonga heading toward her. One look at his concerned expression, and she asked, "What's wrong?"

"It's the other Jupiter whales," Kayonga said. "Both sides are apparently growing restless. Lykohnel's ability to talk to them over distances is fading, and they're apparently growing impatient. They've started moving toward her."

"So we have to get Vicari to her as soon as possible. What does Dr. Vargas say about that?"

Kayonga rubbed the back of his head. "She says it's risky — but it's Vicari's decision."

"That part's easy — he wants to go. Apparently making that contact is some sort of ecstatic experience for him."

Kayonga said, "I'll get the shuttle ready."

———

Carrie watched alongside Kayonga as Vicari slowly made his way down the corridor toward the shuttle *Elaine Shackleton*. He was just learning how to walk using his smart-metal exoskeleton. At first, each step was a clumsy process of slowly lifting one leg while trying to maintain balance with the other, then leaning forward just a bit while making sure that leg made contact with the floor soon enough that he didn't take a tumble.

Carrie told Kayonga, "This would be a lot quicker if we just had a gurney take him."

Kayonga said, "He wanted to make sure he could move around once we landed on top of Lykohnel again. Better to figure that out now."

"I suppose I can't argue with that. Do we know how she's doing?"

"Not good. And the other groups of whales are about half a day away from her. If she's not up to negotiating — things could look bad."

Carrie took another look as Vicari went *clump-clump-clump* down the corridor. "We'll get him there — and he'll make things right."

Once they got Vicari into the passenger seat of the shuttle, Carrie took her place in the co-pilot's position next to Kayonga. *Please forgive me, Adriana,* was her first thought as the shuttle lifted from Callisto Base. *I'm sorry Vicari won't die a slower, more painful death. But at least he's doing something good with what's left of his sorry life.*

———

"The growl of the thunder increased steadily while I looked at him, distinct and black, planted solidly upon the shores of a sea of light. At the moment of greatest brilliance the darkness leaped back with a culminating crash, and he vanished before my dazzled eyes as utterly as though he had been blown to atoms."

-- Joseph Conrad, Lord Jim

———

Then, the now-familiar trip — into the clouds of hydrogen and helium, the massive lightning bolts intermittently lighting the way, sensors probing through the interference from Jupiter's magnetic field, and finally: the initial contact with Lykohnel. "How are you, my friend?" was Kayonga's immediate question.

"I am not well," came the reply, and Carrie believed she could hear how weak the whale's "voice" was even over the datalink translation.

Carrie looked at Kayonga, and his furrowed forehead and narrow-lipped expression showed her the depths of his concern.

From behind Carrie, Vicari asked, "How soon will we get to her?"

"Just about ten minutes," Kayonga replied.

Carrie expected Vicari to make a followup remark, but he remained silent. She thought, *I suppose looking ahead to the last meaningful act you'll do before you die would focus your mind.*

They repeated the process from the previous rendezvous with Lykohnel — hovered over her, allowed her to approach them, and once the shuttle sat safely upon her back, they deployed the contact module.

Vicari's first attempt to rise from his seat was clumsy, and he fell back down into the chair. Carrie, without thinking, offered her hand to help him up. Vicari sat up straight and told her, "Thank you, Carrie. But I intend to do this myself."

Fine, Carrie thought, *See if I care if you fall flat on your ass.*

Vicari's second attempt to stand was still wobbly, but finally he got to his feet, his exoskeleton clanking and whirring. Carrie opened the inner, then outer, airlock hatches, and preceded Vicari onto the surface of Lykohnel's back.

Vicari negotiated his steps more smoothly than Carrie would have anticipated. Kayonga followed. Vicari didn't waste any time, but went down on one knee as he had previously and placed his hands upon Lykohnel's back. Again, he closed his eyes and bowed his head.

In the next instant, Vicari grimaced in pain, and Carrie held her breath, hoping not to witness a repeat of before, with Vicari's body seizing up, threatening Lykohnel's recovery.

After a few more moments, Vicari groaned, and went to both knees, and it looked as if he were struggling to keep his hands placed against Lykohnel's back.

"Let me do this," Vicari pleaded, and Carrie realized he was speaking directly to Lykohnel. "I can help you if you let me do this."

Carrie thought, *If he can't succeed this time, what happens to Lykohnel? And how many other Jupiter whales might die?* She went to him. "Is there anything I can do to help?"

Vicari raised his head, but didn't open his eyes. "Lykohnel is resisting me."

Kayonga came to them and asked, "Why?"

"I can only do so much right here to try to heal her. To save her, I have to become part of her."

Carrie demanded, "What the hell are you talking about?"

Through clenched teeth, Vicari said, "The moment in the infirmary when you thought I was asleep — I was modifying my nanotech. I'd been working on it all day. I can transfer it — and my consciousness — into Lykohnel."

Kayonga looked at Carrie. "Is that possible?"

Carrie said, "The one thing Vicari has never been is a liar. Certainly I'd say he believes what he's saying — whether it's true or not."

Kayonga asked Vicari, "Is Lykohnel resisting you?"

"She is," Vicari said. "She knows I'd be sacrificing my Human body — she won't accept that sacrifice. You have to convince her I'm sincere."

Carrie had a sudden realization, anger flared within her, and she kneeled down next to Vicari. "You want to recapture that feeling you had during your previous contact with Lykohnel. If you're going to die, you want to die happy!"

Vicari fought to open his eyes and glare at Carrie. He said, "I want more than that — I want to live! I can transfer my consciousness into Lykohnel. I can live as long as she does — which could be another century or more."

Carrie grabbed Vicari's arm beneath the exoskeleton. He put up no resistance. "This is bullshit. You don't care a good goddam about her — only for yourself."

"You'd better modify that attitude if you want Lykohnel saved. She knows my attitude toward her, she knows I'd never hurt her. But she also knows everything else about me — she knows about Adriana, she knows how much you hate me."

"So she wants a reference from me?"

"Both my life and Lykohnel's are at stake. Here's what it comes down to — do you hate me more than you want to save her?"

Carrie raised shaking hands toward Vicari's neck. *What I want*, Carrie thought, *is to crush the life out of you.*

Kayonga took a step toward her.

But Carrie's next thought stilled her hands: *What would*

Adriana think of all this? She was always better than me. She'd find a way to reach out with love and understanding.

Carrie placed her hands on her knees. "Lykohnel — do you hear me? Can you understand me?"

"I can," came the response over Carrie's datalink.

"If you trust Vicari to save you, then you should do this. You have to live."

"I do not wish to harm your sister's memory."

"You won't," Carrie said. "No one could ever do that. Not even Malcolm Vicari has done that. By working to keep your people from fighting, you will give her the greatest honor."

No response for a moment.

"This is what Adriana would have wanted," Carrie said. "Please believe me."

Lykohnel said, "Vicari — do what you wish."

Vicari laid himself upon Lykohnel's back, his hands like claws trying to grip the smooth surface of her skin. His body, despite being paralyzed, began to shake within its exoskeleton. *Another seizure!* Carrie thought, and when she looked more closely saw that the exoskeleton's automatic systems were injecting medication into his arm.

That didn't halt the progress of the seizure — but Carrie watched as Vicari's entire body began to glow. She squinted against the increasing intensity of the light emanating from Vicari's body, she raised her hands to shield her face against the heat coming from him, but her legs seemed to freeze in place. She felt hands grabbing her shoulders — Kayonga! — and he pulled her toward the far end of the module as Vicari's body became more amorphous by the moment, until his exoskeleton clattered onto Lykohnel's back.

The glow from Vicari's body began to fade, and as Carrie looked more closely, she understood why — it was as if he were being absorbed into the Jupiter whale's body. Within an instant, she could perceive Vicari only as a glowing presence just beneath the surface of Lykohnel's skin, one that became fainter and fainter.

Carrie stood staring at Vicari's vacant exoskeleton, the only evidence that he'd once occupied that space. It was Kayonga who managed the first words to the Jupiter whale: "Lykohnel, are you all right? Has Vicari begun to heal you?"

Carrie heard a burst of static at first, the Lykohnel's translated voice: "I am becoming well. And Malcolm Vicari — he is here with me."

"The son of a bitch," Carrie muttered.

"Does he live alongside you?" Kayonga asked. "Can he speak to us?"

"He cannot. He is a part of me. Carrie — I understand him fully now. I perceive the depths of the broken parts of him. But my consciousness is much larger than his own. He is here, but he does not command."

Carrie asked, "Does he . . . what does he feel? Does he enjoy the link he has with you?"

Lykohnel replied, "I know how he described his earlier feelings. He described them accurately. It is, for him, as transcendent as he described. He is happy beyond Human measure."

Kayonga asked, "Will you continue to heal properly?"

"I will. By the time each group of my own species arrives here, I will be in excellent shape to continue negotiations."

Carrie started toward the airlock. All she could manage to say was, "The best of luck to you, Lykohnel. If we can do anything else for you, let us know."

Carrie sat in silence on the way back to Callisto Station, helping Kayonga monitor the shuttle's systems, and keeping an eye on sensor readouts.

———

Once back at Callisto Base, Carrie asked Kayonga to her tiny quarters where they sat on a couch in the small living area and shared a bottle of wine. She told him what Vicari had explained about the nature of his ecstatic emotions. "I understand the feelings of love he compared them to. Just being in his mother's presence, or even anticipating seeing her. I felt the same thing for my father, even in the last moment I spent with him, as he was dying."

Kayonga said, "I've always felt that with my brother, Omari. We shared so much. Playing with toy spaceships as children. Helping each other study at university. And party."

"And Vicari claimed to understand the feelings of religionists for God, even though he wasn't one."

Kayonga leaned forward and took a sip of wine. "Ironic, that."

"I suppose. Just before I took Vicari into custody three years ago, he used his abilities against me. Took my sense of irony."

Kayonga leaned back in the couch. "I guess that's also kind of — "

"I wouldn't know!"

"Sorry."

"It's fine," Carrie said. "Either way, I'm not a religionist, either. Not like you are."

"I only know what I feel."

"What, uh, sect are you?"

"I am a sect, as you say, of one. My feeling of God comes from standing at the edge of the ocean on Beyin Beach, looking up, and trying to count the stars."

"That sounds beautiful. No really, don't look at me that way, it does. I've never experienced that feeling, but I'm glad you have." Carrie took a sip of her own glass before she continued: "Now, the sexual part of what Vicari spoke about, that I know something about."

Kayonga stared at her over his own glass. "I see."

"Does your sense of God keep you from . . . "

Kayonga smiled. "My 'sect' has no arbitrary rules about how we celebrate God's gift of our bodies."

"Then put the glass down." Carrie led him into the bedroom. They barely had their clothing off before Carrie took Kayonga by the shoulders, pressed him down upon the bed, and straddled him.

They moved clumsily at first, in the way of first-time lovers, but soon found their rhythm. But even as the intensity of their lovemaking grew, and her moment drew near, Carrie began to weep, knowing these feelings of affection and sexual attraction were nothing compared to the feelings of love, spirituality, and physical release Malcolm Vicari was experiencing right now within Lykohnel's consciousness, that he would continue to feel day after day after day, quite likely into the next century.

Finding Chidera

Editors Frank Hall and Robin Blankenship were looking for stories for an anthology titled DYSTOPIAN EXPRESS. I'm kind of burned out on dystopian stories, but I suggested a tale that could be the final one in the book, with a more optimistic take on the genre. That led to the following story, "Finding Chidera."

———

Chidera Kapur fights his way out of exhausted sleep. Twenty-seven hours awake, most of them under interrogation. His head lolls. Strikes something hard and flat. Eyes flutter open. Beneath him, the Earth is in flames.

His mind struggles toward full awareness. Mouth feels dusty. *I'm on a shuttle*, he remembers. *Headed through the fires of re-entry. Everyone keeps reminding me the Earth is our original home, wondering why I wouldn't want to go there for the first time. I feel like I'm returning to the womb within a veil of fire.*

Around him, people ooh and ahh, their faces cast in a

devilish light. *Not appropriate,* Chidera thinks, *it's the hell of the New Lancaster Habitat that I'm leaving.*

Memories of that hell sear through his consciousness despite a determined effort to cast his mind away from them. Getting by during the last decade, from the time he was a newly orphaned pre-teen, has meant performing any job demanded in Gideon Markham's restaurant or a good beating followed. Sometimes it followed anyway.

Spend hours cleaning toilets and be beaten for being dirty. Report to the main dining hall and have boiling soup dumped on him by "accident" in front of paying customers, who loved "practical jokes."

Be forced to lick boots to all-around laughter. Sixteen-hour, 18-hour days, more beatings at the slightest infraction, real or imagined.

All on an Earth-orbital habitat that could've had all those duties performed by scrupulously clean, tireless tech.

But that wasn't the point. The point was being able to lord it over someone, to be privileged in a time when tech had abolished privilege throughout much of Human space.

And now I'm free, he thinks.

Of all but my own guilt.

———

Final approach to the city of Brussels: Chidera squints against sunlight as it mirrors off glass-walled skyscrapers, opens eyes wide again to take in constant movement — flitters zooming across the sky, monorails cruising just over street level, pedestrians scurrying ant-like among buildings.

My world is opening up, he thinks. *Soon to be more than filthy back rooms and constant humiliation.*

Never mind that he'd brought humiliation upon himself in his final moments back on the habitat.

Religious leaders on New Lancaster, which was primarily populated by New Order Mennonites, had discovered Markham's abuses and, with the help of Earth Unity security, shut his place down. Chidera, freed of his servitude, could choose: remain on the habitat or settle on Earth.

He chose Earth, but his best friend — only friend, Miyanda Mukela — begged him to remain. He tried, but couldn't push aside memories of all the times they'd commiserated with one another far into the night, aching for the chance to share more than a furtive kiss before the threat of the master's fists sent them to their separate rooms.

As they stood outside the restaurant within the two-kilometer wide cylinder, she threw herself into his arms, telling him, "I'll be all alone here, you gotta stay!"

Chidera closed his eyes tightly against her words, wanting to scatter them to the winds. Freedom was his only thought, and if leaving behind the misery and the pain meant also leaving behind his only source of solace and comfort, then so be it.

He held Miyanda by the shoulders until she whimpered in pain. "I can't stay here any longer," he told her. "Come with me."

Miyanda looked as frightened as she ever had beneath Gideon Markham's stern gaze. "No, I — I can't! This is . . . home!"

"No longer my home," Chidera told her. "No longer mine. I have to make a new life." He relaxed his grip on her shoulders, turned, and started walking, Miyanda's cries fading with every step.

———

Shining, sparkling all-white room within Earth Unity head-quarters, inside the old European Parliament building. Silvery table, a sterile smell. Two women insist Chidera undress, no need to be embarrassed, they're doctor and nurse, medical checkup is just routine.

Bare ass on table, expect a shock of cold, but it's surpris-ingly warm. Maybe even calibrated to his body temp. Neither woman touches him at first. One runs a hand scanner across his body as the other checks readouts on a medical console. Chidera discretely folds his hands across his groin, and the doctor gives him a knowing grin.

Despite their professionalism and friendly manner, Chidera fears these women, as he does anyone in authority. *I feel as if a trap door is about to open beneath me at any moment,* he thinks.

From casual conversation he picked up while aboard the shuttle, he realizes that apparently Earth has recently suffered from an attack by aliens called the Jenregar, which disrupted much of the worldwide network of maglev train, but that's been repaired now. He saw no evidence of such a conflict among the tall, beautiful buildings of Brussels.

"Mr. Kapur," the doctor says, "you're in excellent health physically. Some scarring on your back. That's something we can take care of right away, if you'd like."

"No," is all he says, and doesn't choose to elaborate. *I'll wear those scars as a badge of honor,* he thinks. Though he wonders if eventually he may change his mind.

The doctor continues: "Psychologically, I expect you should be able to adjust well enough to Earth. It's very different from what you're used to, of course. But it's also better in every way. Replicator economy. Essential needs taken care of. Housing, food, clothing, all that."

"I've heard. Sounds like paradise."

"You might want to schedule some counseling, all the same. This can be a rough transition."

"I'll consider that."

One final procedure, he's told. They will insert a device called a datalink just under his skin. It's a microscopic implant that, as far as he can tell, serves as a combination communications device and tracking system. It can even translate the speech of the Galactic intelligences that Humanity has regular contact with.

The doctor asks him to stand still as she places the barrel of a device that looks disturbingly like a pistol just behind his left ear. She pulls the trigger. Chidera flinches, as much from anticipation as anything; the sting is minimal.

The examination ends. Chidera's given a clean bill of health and a new set of clothing. His old dirty and, no doubt, unfashionable work shirt and durable pants have been discarded. His new shirt is shiny and white, with a tall collar. It abrades his skin, and his hand keeps rising without thinking to rub the back of his neck. His pants appear to conform themselves to his waistline; he has no belt.

And no pockets. *Where do I keep my stuff,* he wonders.

———

Chidera's departure from the medical unit is unremarkable; he's told his new home, at least for now, will be a town called Encinitas, which is apparently in a North American province called California, which he believes he's heard of.

He's guided to a large elevator crammed with a couple dozen or so people, and heads downward to the Brussels-Luxembourg Railway Station beneath Unity HQ. The people all around him waiting to go about their business, whatever that might be, seem happy and healthy enough, and some nod in friendly acknowledgement as the elevator descends.

Elevator doors slide open. A whiff of air enters the elevator car. Oddly, it smells fresher than the air outside or in the medical unit.

Chidera pauses. The wave of people from the elevator car parts and flows around him. This station doesn't resemble anything he expected. He sees nothing resembling a rail line, no metal rails over an endless string of wooden ties. He wonders if his impression of such a place is too informed by historical documentaries and dramas.

Immediately before him, people are lined up against a solid wall beneath a gray domed roof. He can make out conversations in French and what he imagines to be Dutch as well as in English. Long corridors to his right and left terminate in similar walls. Escalators and elevators take people to levels above and below this one. On a whim, he takes a right to investigate down that corridor.

And hears a voice inside his head!

"Chidera Kapur — the maglev train you are scheduled to use lies straight ahead," the voice tells him.

He stops cold. Pivots slowly on one heel to face forward again. Of course. The datalink. Sees all. Knows his every move. No escape, any more than he could escape his captivity back in the habitat. What would happen, he wonders, if he were to continue to the right?

Anyway. Stand stock still. Face forward. Wait.

Within moments, he feels a low rumble beneath his feet, but doesn't hear the train's approach. Wouldn't such a train make its very mass, its substance, more apparent?

Perhaps not. Certainly people around Chidera seem expectant. Around him, here's a man rolling his shoulders, a woman checking her wrist readout, another man bouncing slightly on his heels, impatient to get going.

The rumbling fades. A pause, as if to add drama. Then the wall raises, and the maglev train is revealed. After all the buildup, it's rather a mundane vehicle, containing a row of seats two across on either side of a single aisle. Chidera travels along with the flow of people and quickly finds a seat. No windows. Then he remembers — of course, there are no windows, because all there would be to see is the inside of a tube. And within that tube, a vacuum, which gives the train its great speed. It's also, he realizes, why he didn't hear the train's approach — sound wouldn't travel within that vacuum.

No one sits next to him. He wonders if he's somehow marked, somehow obviously different from those around him, and they're spurning him. His next thought is how ludicrous the previous thought was; it's simply not crowded on this train, and people tend to create their own private spaces, given the opportunity.

How far away is California? he wonders. Chidera realizes there's a fold-down comp on the seat in front of him. Fold it down. Ask a question, in a low voice: "How far is it from Brussels to Encinitas?"

The comp, in a pleasant female voice, replies, "Nine thousand, ninety-three point one kilometers."

Chidera's eyes widen and he fidgets in his seat. Over nine thousand K! This trip could take days, he realizes, and wonders if he should have stocked up on provisions for this trip.

But I have no money, is his next thought, and then he remembers most places on Earth, unlike New Lancaster Habitat, do not have a market economy. Replicators are everywhere, and to Chidera it's as if magic has become real.

Calm down. Ask the obvious question. "How long will this trip take?"

"Approximately one and one-half hours."

How is that possible, Chidera asks himself. *I haven't even felt the train start to move.* "Has this train started up yet?"

"We are nearing our first stop — London."

Chidera takes a deep breath. "How far have we come in this trip?"

"Approximately 360 kilometers."

"How long did that take us?"

"Approximately five minutes, including acceleration and deceleration."

Chidera grips his seat's armrests in anger. *Someone believes I'm a fool,* he thinks. *I'm sitting in a stationary train car, denied windows, and expected to think I'm shooting across the European continent.*

The car's doors open. Passengers file out as others wait to enter. The station beyond those doors is different from the one he supposedly left in Brussels, the roof still a dome, but lower, and an odd shade of beige rather than gray. Now all the conversations around him are in English, and these new passengers' mode of dress and even their gestures have subtly changed.

Chidera slumps into his seat, his anger rising. Arms folded, jaw set. He's confused, as he can't imagine someone would create all the stage sets needed to deceive him in this way, or create a virtual reality program for that purpose.

But something has happened, he thinks as the doors shut him off from "London." And although he intends to ride this trip out, once he arrives in "Encinitas," he intends to demand answers.

New York City. St. Louis. Denver. Beyond the first city, Chidera has little concept of the exact location of the others, but he knows they are placed across the width of the North American continent. Yet each trip takes only minutes to achieve. At San Diego, California, the stop is a bit longer than at the others.

Chidera reasons that if he is already in California, the trip to Encinitas cannot take much longer. Sure enough, when the doors finally close at San Diego, it's only a matter of about half a minute before they open again.

Chidera's datalink tells him: "You have reached your destination. Welcome to Encinitas, California." The doors open onto a smaller station than he's seen before, this being the only track visible. A pale woman who looks to be in her late twenties or early thirties comes up to him. "Chidera Kapur?" Her smile appears sincere to Chidera, but it doesn't seem to extend to the lines at the corners of her eyes.

"Yes." He draws close to the woman, thrusting a finger toward her face. "I demand to know what's going on."

The woman's expression doesn't change. "I'm Helena Penner. I'm to be your guide during your first days here."

Chidera takes another step toward Helena. "And just where is 'here?' Am I still in Brussels?"

Helena takes a deep breath. "Another centimeter closer, and I can put you on the floor. Then police officers will take you away."

Chidera realizes his breathing is rapid. He fears he may be hyperventilating. Between breaths, he manages to say, "Already, the threats have begun."

"You made the first one. Now, come with me or get on the next train back to Brussels."

Chidera stands, eyes closed tight, breath huffing, fists clenched.

Helena continues: "If you'll just come outside with me, I can prove you're really in California."

With effort, fists unclench. Breathing slows. Eyes open. "All right. Take me."

Helena turns and starts up a short flight of stairs. Chidera rushes to follow her. As they near the top of the stairs, Chidera's eyes narrow and he raises a hand against bright sunlight. They emerge on a cliff about a hundred meters above a beach that stretches as far as he can see in either direction. Surfers perform their balancing acts upon the more challenging waves. Directly below, children scream in delight.

The ocean breeze is salty and cool.

Chidera nearly staggers from an overload of sights and sounds. Ocean and sky seem to reach toward infinity. Chidera realizes in a flash how accustomed he is to being enclosed and secure within the comforting curve of a habitat's interior.

Helena asks, "Have you ever seen a virt this good?"

"I've hardly ever been in one."

"Pick up a rock. Any good-sized rock."

"What the hell are you — "

"Pick it up, goddam it!"

Habit and instinct kick in, and, hating himself for it, Chidera picks up a fist-sized rock.

Helena gives him a hard stare. "Hit yourself in the head with it."

"What the hell?"

"I'm proving you're not in a virt. Knock some sense into your own brain."

Chidera taps the rock against his head.

"Harder!"

Again, a tap.

"Harder!"

He knocks himself on the head, harder this time. "Damn!"

he says, and drops the rock. "I should'a tossed that at your head."

"Which wouldn't prove anything if I was a virt just like everything else you saw. Have you ever heard of a virt where you can hurt yourself?"

"I guess I haven't." Chidera folds his hands and performs a slight bow. "I apologize. Please forgive me."

"No trouble at all," Helena says. "This is my job."

"I thought people on Earth didn't have jobs."

"Most of us don't have to. Some of us want to."

"And you're one of those people."

"I'm also from New Lancaster Habitat. I got out a couple of years ago."

"I never knew you from Gideon Markham's restaurant."

"I was never there," Helena says. "I was in the majority area — the Mennonite area. I worked in the fields on my parents' farm. I knew Malcolm Vicari."

"Oh," is all Chidera can say at first. Vicari was a sexual predator who misused medical biotech to steal others' emotions and relive them anytime he wanted, often leaving his victims empty shells mentally. "I'm sorry."

"I was actually one of the luckier ones. No permanent physical harm. My mind's still intact. But unfortunately, so are all the memories of what he did to me. Yeah. Damn lucky."

"I don't know what to say. I don't know which is worse. The beatings I took or . . . "

"Let's not make it a competition, OK? Lemme get you settled into your house."

Helena starts walking away, realizes Chidera isn't following, and turns. "What?" she asks.

Chidera can only say, "House?"

Helena opens her arms wide in front of a small, plain, single-story concrete home overlooking a nearly deserted stretch of beach. To Chidera, it may as well have been a palace.

"I . . . live here?" he asks. "All by myself?"

Helena turns, and this time her smile is more impressive. "All by yourself! Let's go inside."

Through the reinforced doorway. House is completely furnished, with hand-crafted furniture, many items made of wood. Living room gives way to kitchen, hallway to the right has doorways leading to two bedrooms and a bath.

The entire time, Helena enthuses over the home, showing him the environmental controls, the replicator, how the house can detect severe weather and harden itself against any threat, even a hurricane, though such storms are rare in California. "There's even a nanodoc module that can detect a medical emergency and send for help even as it's treating you," she says.

I might need that doc in a minute, Chidera thinks, as the room starts to spin and he grabs the back of a chair.

Helena, not noticing his distress, throws open the doors to the back of the house, which boasts a deck that looks out upon a different stretch of ocean and beach. Chidera manages to take a tentative step onto the deck, and the air, still cool, settles his senses. The dizziness fades.

The sun is lower in the sky now. The waves caress the beach with less force here. "Looks like I can have a lot of privacy," Chidera tells Helena.

"You sure can."

"Why does anyone live anywhere else than Earth?"

Helena looks out across the waters. Chidera suspects she isn't paying much attention to them. "Earth isn't perfect, by any means," she says. "You might find that freedom has its own traps."

Chidera considers that. "I get that. I think I could name you more than one person who would just sit around drunk all day."

Helena leans against the deck's sturdy railing. "Sad thing is, you really could do that, and your home's nanodoc would just clear out all the toxins the next day, and send out some biotech to prevent cardiomyopathy and cirrhosis of the liver. And it wouldn't let you leave while you're impaired. Second attempt brings actual people to help."

"Help? You mean the police."

"No. Counseling if you want it. If underlying psychological factors are making you drink, they can let you talk through it until you're cured. If that won't work, they might even be able to do a snip in your brain."

Chidera's horrified. "They'd operate on your brain?"

"Only if that's what you wanted, and only if you had parts you wanted to forget — stuff that was leading you to the drinking or drug use or becoming a virthead, or whatever."

"There's nothing like that happening with me."

Helena stares out at the ocean for a long moment, then asks Chidera, "Did you receive an offer of psychological counseling?"

"Yes."

"Yes, and — ?"

"I turned it down."

"Typical."

"What?"

"Chidera, I'm just remembering having to tell you to back off. There's anger there that could become dangerous to someone. Maybe even yourself. Maybe especially yourself."

"I'll . . . I'll be fine."

Helena's face breaks out in a mischievous smile. She tells him, "Just wait. It's easy to think you've arrived in paradise.

But even watching the waves roll in and drinking margaritas can get boring after awhile."

"Is that why you have this job?"

"It's one reason. That, and wanting to help people who've escaped from New Lancaster. Or any number of other places where they've been beaten, abused . . . raped. You know."

"Yeah."

"Some of those places are still right here on Earth."

"Standing in this house, that's hard to believe."

"Believe it. Well, then, I guess I'll leave you to enjoy your home."

Chidera looks around. "That's it?"

"That's it. If you need anything, you can give me a call on your datalink."

"I guess I'm confused."

"It's common. When I first arrived here on Earth, I stayed curled up in my bed for a week."

Chidera takes a step. "I — " Now he does stagger.

Helena starts to reach for him, but stills her hand just short of touching him. "Whoa, hold up! You all right?"

"Yeah. Just . . . sleepy. Hungry."

"I've been a fool. Of course you are. Lemme get you started on a meal."

Chidera follows her toward the kitchen.

Helena asks, "What do you want?"

Sit at the table. Time to test the home's capabilities. "Well . . . steak would be nice. If we have it."

"We have whatever you can dream up," Helena says. Works the replicator unit. "How'd you like it?"

"Well done. Baked potato?"

"Coming right up."

"Tea?"

"Tea, we've got as well."

Chidera's eyelids flutter. Chin sinks toward chest. Then: sharp aroma of cooked meat. Earthy, salty smell of potato. Clinking sound of ice falling into a glass, then of tea pouring against the ice.

Helena sets the plate before him, and Chidera can barely believe the sight. It's as fantastic as the shuttle flight downward to the Earth or the crashing of the waves against the California shore.

He devours his food, savoring the easy way his knife slides through the steak as much as the flavor of the meat itself. The interior of the potato is as fluffy as freshly-fallen snow, the butter melted within it just arrived from heaven. The tea is beyond nectar.

This is how all those I served for so many years lived, he thinks. *All the food they wanted, live where they like, have as many friends as they wanted.*

He holds up a finger to capture Helena's attention. Swallows a too-big, though delicious, lump of food. "Show me again how to work that. You know, for in the morning."

Helena shows him, then says, "I'll leave you alone to enjoy your meal. Some more immigrants are coming in over the next few days, and I'll be their guide as well. But I'll try to see how you're doing."

"Thanks," Chidera says, food muffling his voice. Helena leaves. He finishes his meal. Sits back, rubs his stomach.

Gets up. Goes to the replicator. Calls up the same thing again. It's just as good the second time.

Double feast done. Chidera lumbers into bed, not even turning it down, wearing all his new clothes. Sleep is immediate, but in his dreams he throws up his arms against the brutal fists of Gideon Markham one moment, and reaches for the gentle hand of Miyanda the next. As far as he can extend his hand, though, it doesn't reach far enough actually to touch her.

———

Rising from sleep. A slow process. Chidera's lying on his back. Urge to pee is great, but so's the urge to keep from having to get up. He realizes only after a few moments that the light cast against the ceiling is natural light — sunshine!

That's right, he recalls. *I'm on Earth. I'm free.*

But to do what?

For now, he decides, *to resign myself to getting up. Gotta pee pretty bad. That pressure's not going away.*

After that, and other morning rituals in the pristine bathroom, time to plan the day.

First things first. Breakfast? Chidera rubs his stomach, recalls making the same gesture last night after stuffing himself. Still. Go to the replicator. Order up a glass of orange juice and a cinnamon pastry. Then to the deck.

Chidera looks toward the sunrise, realizes he has to have slept about twelve hours. Quite a luxury.

A sip of juice, and his body finally seems to get the message that it has to move today. I should go into town, Chidera thinks. Engage with people. After all, I'm all alone here.

He pushes thoughts of Miyanda aside as he heads out the door.

———

The town, it turns out, isn't far from Chidera's home. Though the air is still, the morning's still cool. Even as he flags down a transit bubble, though, he can feel the sun asserting itself, making it clear that the day will keep growing warmer. While boarding the single-passenger bubble, he makes a mental note to find out how to access a weather forecast, something unneeded within the habitat. He thinks, *I'd also better check what kind of variation in weather this province has. My home can harden itself against hurricanes, Helena told me. She said they're rare, but that doesn't mean one couldn't arrive in the next few days? What else might I have to endure? Floods? Snow? Earthquakes?*

As the bubble glides along the center of a grassy roadway, he encounters joggers, most of whom give him a friendly nod. He begins to get a feel for which people are probably locals and which are likely tourists.

One couple — or is it a foursome? — Chidera sees walking toward the ocean are certainly tourists. The two are Cetronen paired symbionts. Each consists of two beings. The "major" is the about two-and-a-half meters tall, with thick fur and muscular arms. They have wide pointed ears, a thin mouth, and no nose. The "minors" are smaller, thinner versions of the same species who sit on a hump on the major's belly. The majors provide the strength, the minors bring the brains.

Chidera has never seen an alien — oops, got to remember that word's taboo here on Earth! — before. He openly stares. He's tempted to speak to them, to give his datalink a workout, to see if they could understand him, and he, them. But he doesn't, and isn't sure why.

Both majors ignore him, intent upon carrying along their minors. One of the minors gives Chidera a stare from deep-set eyes beneath a jutting brow. He wishes he could read the emotional content of that stare.

Who thought I'd ever live in a tourist spot, he thinks. *Somewhere a person, even someone from another planet, of another species, would* want *to go to.*

And tourist spots, he thinks, *will have restaurants.* The idea has an immediate appeal. From stuffing himself the night before, he already knows how enjoyable the food here on Earth can be.

What would it be like to be waited on, rather than being the servant?

His heart races with excitement at the prospect — he could be the one giving the orders, he could be the one looking down upon someone, forcing them to —

No.

Shame washes over him, and he hopes it isn't visible on his face to the people he's passing. *How could I even consider that?* he wonders. *I know what humiliating someone else is like. I know how I felt about those who made me lick their boots or who watched when I became the butt of a so-called joke.*

Why would I ever want to be that person?

He continues toward town, the very idea, and the shame associated with it, fading only slowly.

When he arrives in the town proper, he's confused. He approaches what appears to be the main street, judging by the large overhead sign reminding him he's in ENCINITAS. The street is mostly a wide pedestrian walkway, but he sees tracks that imply trolley cars also run here.

But he has to wonder where all the businesses are. To his right, he sees residential buildings that could be either large homes or small hotels. To the left, what appears to be a public swimming pool. This close to the beach? Plenty of people are walking around, but where the hell are they going?

Where are the restaurants? Where are the gift shops?

Then Chidera realizes: I'm taking my cues from living on the habitat, and from watching historical cube dramas. No market economy here.

Damn. A world without restaurants? Hard to imagine.

Chidera continues down the street. People passing the other way flash a smile or say, "Hello," and he reciprocates. A trolley, sure enough, rounds a corner, gliding almost soundlessly down the tracks until its bell sounds out with repeated dings as its operator gives Chidera a big wave.

Finally! He approaches a storefront with tables and chairs out front. Is this outside seating for a restaurant?

He exits the bubble and looks at a sign overhead. Turn the Key is apparently the name of the place. Chidera leans toward the front window and cups his hands against the glass to see inside. Plenty of tables, chairs, and booths indicating a restaurant. He sees a menu attached to the store's glass front. He takes a look: various pizzas, antipasto, chicken and veal dishes. "Oh — Italian," he says aloud without realizing it.

A voice behind him: "You'll have to come join us sometime."

Chidera turns and finds himself facing a man in his fifties, dark hair going gray, with clear blue eyes and a broad smile.

Perplexed at being caught talking to himself, Chidera can only say, "What?"

"You'll have to join us sometime for a meal. I promise you the best."

"Are you . . . the owner?"

The man shakes Chidera's hand. "I have that honor. "Tremaine Keyes."

Chidera indicates the overhead sign. "But you're not open?"

"Not right now."

"When are you open?"

Tremaine shrugs. "I don't know. I have to get in the mood, maybe come up with some dishes I haven't done before."

"You mean — "

Tremaine snapped his fingers. "You haven't been to Earth before. I bet you came from a market economy."

"You'd be right about that," Chidera says, grateful that he didn't have to go into the full explanation.

"Well, the fortunate thing is that I can set my own working hours. The hard part is getting some help. I love making food for people, but I can't do all the preparation by myself. And someone has to be wait staff, and it can be hard to find volunteers for that."

"Well, Mr. Keyes — "

"Please, make it Tremaine."

"Very well. Tremaine. I'll be sure to check back sometime to see when you might be open."

"You do that. I'll look forward to it."

As he walks away, Chidera thinks, *I heard the implied recruitment pitch, but I'll be damned if I'll volunteer to do something that used to pay me in beatings and humiliation.*

———

Chidera wanders through much of the town but doesn't find another restaurant. Small public food replicator facilities are scattered throughout the community, some even with seating, but they seem impersonal, sterile to him.

But safe, he realizes. It also occurs to him he's seen no police officers, no security guards, no officials of any sort the entire time. *These people can't be that goddam perfect,* he thinks. *Someone has to beat the shit out of someone every once in a while. Someone has to . . . well, I guess they don't have theft in a place where you can have anything you want.*

Maybe Helena's right. Maybe paradise gets boring.

As if thinking of her conjured her up, Helena's voice

comes over Chidera's datalink. "How's your first full day on Earth?"

"Thinking about what you said yesterday. How'd you like a margarita?"

"Sounds great, actually."

"I'm headed back to my house. Let's meet on the beach."

"See you soon," Helena says, and signs off.

———

Back to the house. Set the replicator for a couple of margaritas. Head down to the beach. He's intrigued by the inexorable rhythm of the waves, by the idea that Earth's moon is their main engine. *I thought I was at the mercy of a habitat for most of my life,* he thinks, *but these waves are at the mercy of an entire world.*

Chidera takes only a couple sips of his drink before Helena catches up to him. He hands her the other drink and she thanks him.

"So how did your day go?"

"I met a restaurant owner."

Helena stops in mid-sip. "Tell me you didn't go looking for restaurants."

"Not as such. But it occurred to me once I got into town."

"This is my fault. That was a rookie mistake on my part."

"I shouldn't go to a restaurant?"

"You shouldn't go to a place that evokes bad memories just because it's something familiar."

"I wanted to be the person being waited on for once."

Helena sighs. "That's just as bad. That's reversing the concept instead of avoiding it. A common pattern."

"Shouldn't I be facing these issues instead of avoiding them?"

Helena takes a long sip. "That's one theory."

"You're not a trained psychologist."

"I'm someone who's been down a lot of the same paths you have."

Chidera takes in a long breath of sea air, watches a phalanx of clouds advancing over the waves. "I don't feel as if I'm entitled to such beauty."

"You're entitled to whatever you can grab. Without hurting someone else."

"Yeah. A new concept to me."

"Paradise isn't for the weak. It can defeat you sure as being a slave or a prisoner can. It fools you because it feels good while it's doing it."

"How do I keep that from happening?"

"Reach out. Create your own community. Find people with common interests. Did you have people you counted on back in New Lancaster?"

(Miyanda's gentle hands wash his wounds after a particularly severe beating.)

He can barely hear his own voice say, "Yes."

"You have to find people like that here."

"Our common interests back there were not getting beaten. I'm sure here you're talking about art or music or something."

"The people you became close to were the ones who just happened to be thrown together with you."

"Yeah."

(Miyanda wraps his wounds and makes sure he gets into bed so he can return to work in four hours.)

Chidera reaches for Helena's hand. She squeezes it in return. Pulls it slowly away.

Chidera looks questioningly at her. Helena says, "I'm sorry. I'm still in the middle of my own recovery."

He understands. Emotional abuse. Sexual abuse.

Helena continues: "I'm leaving here soon, anyway."

Blood pulses at Chidera's neck. "Where are you going?"

"Just away. You have your common pattern. I have mine. I'm going to travel all around North America. Maybe even other continents."

"And that's common among — "

"Among people who get the hell out of habitats to make a better life down here. Yes."

"I . . . hope it goes well for you."

Helena smiles. "I do, too. You'll get another guide."

"But you'll come back?"

Helena looks at Chidera. Her expression reveals little. "I hope so. But it has to be what's best for me."

"That's how it should be. And maybe something I need to learn, too."

Helena hands Chidera her margarita glass. She turns away from the beach, and Chidera starts to follow, but she holds up a hand and he stops. "No," she tells him. "You'll see me before I go. Right now, I think it's best for you to stand right here and convince yourself you deserve this beauty."

Chidera faces the ocean again. He hears Helena padding away. He only turns to look back at her a couple of times before she's gone.

———

Over the next three days: Chidera watches the entire 18-hour-long cube saga A SHADOW OF HONOR, based on Rosa Sandage's classic work on the Great Human War, which was fought nearly a half-century earlier. Tires of steak. Tries Chinese, Somali, Thai, and Guatemalan dishes. Stands on the beach for hours at at a time, watching the sun advance across the sky, the eternal lapping of the waves. Drinks more margaritas.

He doesn't shower for two of those days.

Helena calls once, but the conversation is short; Chidera doesn't feel like talking, and she's obviously busy getting ready to leave on her journey, or quest, or however she thinks of it.

Perhaps I don't deserve paradise, he thinks on the fourth morning. *I certainly haven't been doing much with it.*

Decision. Time for a shower, first. Then head back toward the town. Destination: exactly where Helena advised him he shouldn't go.

Turn the Key, this time, is apparently open. No customers visible through the front window, but he can see movement inside.

His hand hesitates mere centimeters from the front door handle. *I don't know why the hell I'm here,* he realizes. *I don't want to work here. And Helena says I shouldn't want to be waited on.*

Chidera pulls his hand back. How the hell did I get so confused? How the hell can there be too much that's good in my life?

Helena was right, he decides. He starts to walk away. Behind him, the restaurant door opens. Tremaine Keyes' voice: "Chidera, where you goin'? We're not quite open yet, but com'on in."

The desire not to be rude overrules all of Chidera's objections. His smile for Tremaine is genuine, and he's quick to accept his handshake.

Tremaine holds the door open for Chidera, slaps his back as Chidera passes through the doorway. "Good to see you. You won't believe what I've come up with for my next dishes." He indicates the rear of the restaurant. "I even lined up some help. In fact, she just came here from some habitat or another, just like you did."

The dining room is only dimly lit. Tremaine motions for him to head toward the rear of the restaurant. A door back there swings open and a woman wearing an apron comes out from the kitchen.

Chidera stops breathing. It's Miyanda!

Then he's rushing toward her. Miyanda's eyes go wide as she looks up and sees him. He reads fear on her face. He realizes he must be silhouetted in this dark room against the stark light from the street, and she may not even recognize him.

A chair stands in his way. He casts it aside. It overturns onto the floor. A table is next, its legs scooting with a screeching sound against the floor.

He reaches Miyanda. That detached part of his mind can't understand why he's ripping the apron off her when he should be sweeping her up in an affectionate embrace. "What the hell are you doing here?" he demands.

A hand clasps his shoulder. Tremaine says, "Get away from her!"

Chidera throws his arm back, thrusting Tremaine's hand away. His unexpected anger still commands him, but he can't allow it to harm Miyanda. The overturned chair is handy. He picks it up, tosses it against the nearest wall. A crash and a clatter, and all his anger is in play as a table becomes his next target, and a couple more chairs go flying, and then he feels a pounding on his face and head and he realizes his wrath has turned against himself and in the next instant the floor rises up to slam against his body.

———

Chidera's first awareness: the voices around him as he lies on the floor, but with someone cradling his bruised and pounding head.

He hears Tremaine: "I've called the medics. They'll be here within a minute."

Miyanda: "What happened to him? I've never seen him like this."

Chidera's eyelids open only reluctantly. It's Miyanda who's holding his head in her lap. "Oh, thank God," she says, "you're awake."

His voice is a painful croak. "I'm . . . I'm sorry. I don't know why I . . . no, wait a minute. That's not true. I know why. I just didn't want to admit it to myself."

"Don't worry about any of that now."

"I have to. I saw you in a position where I'd only seen you abused. I didn't want that to happen anymore. But this is a different place."

"Everybody says it's paradise."

"It is. But it isn't perfect. And neither am I."

The medics, a man and a woman, arrive. They ask Tremaine to step back but tell Miyanda she can continue to hold Chidera. Both run hand scanners over him. Chidera recalls the medical checkup upon first arriving on Earth. *At least they didn't make me get naked,* he thinks.

As the female medic runs another instrument over him, Chidera asks Miyanda, "How did you even get here?"

"I wanted to surprise you." Tears flow down Miyanda's cheeks. "I guess I did."

"And in the first moment I see you . . . I do this."

"You didn't hurt me. I was scared *for* you. But I wasn't scared *of* you."

Chidera's pain subsides. He touches his face, expecting it to be swollen and tender, but it's not. "You'll be fine, Mr. Kapur," the male medic tells him. "But I see Helena Penner is your guide. I think it'd be best if you have a long talk with her, whether here or, well, in custody."

Miyanda speaks up: "I'm not pressing any charges."

"Neither am I," says Tremaine.

"Very well, then," the medic says. He tells Chidera, "Take it easy for a couple days."

The medics leave. Chidera tells Tremaine, "Thanks, both of you, for not . . . you know."

Miyanda says, "I only wanted to help you."

Tremaine kneels next to him. Touches his arm. "Don't worry about it. I'm just glad you weren't more seriously hurt."

"It's your restaurant that took all the damage," Chidera says.

"And I'm going to insist that you help clean up."

Chidera sits up, rubs his head. "I'll do that gladly."

"Good. Then I don't want to see either you or Miyanda in here for a long time."

Miyanda's jaw drops. "But, Mr. Keyes, I need this job."

"It's Tremaine. And no, you don't. Not here. And part of this is my fault. If I'd looked into your background, Miyanda, I'd never have let you in here. For your own good."

Chidera rises. He pulls Miyanda up. She asks, "But what'll we do?"

Chidera says, "I think I know."

Tremaine looks into Chidera's face and nods. "I can see you've figured it out."

Chidera slaps Tremaine on the shoulder. "Let's start cleaning up, first."

———

Afterward, Chidera takes Miyanda to show off his home. She stands in the middle of his living room and spins around. "All this is yours?"

"Didn't they give you a home yet?"

Miyanda stops spinning. Her expression turns serious. "I just got here from Brussels. I . . . told them I hoped I didn't need a home."

Chidera goes to her. "Because you wanted to come here."

"I do," Miyanda says, and they embrace. After a moment, they kiss.

Chidera, smiling, looks all around. Miyanda, seeing that, looks worried. "What is it?"

Chidera laughs. "No one to look out for. We're free."

Another embrace. Miyanda pulls him into the bedroom.

Chidera's hand trembles as he touches her bare skin for the first time. "Just take it slow," Miyanda tells him.

Finding the proper positioning of arms and legs is awkward at first. Laughter cures that. What follows is tentative, then frantic, then joyous.

The second time is ever better and becomes the template for the rest of the night.

———

Chidera, Miyanda, and Helena stand in the Encinitas maglev station, in front of the wide doorway behind which the maglev train will arrive soon. Helena stands next to her luggage. Chidera and Miyanda are here to see her off on her journey.

Helena tells Chidera, "I don't think this could've worked out better. Except that I should've insisted upon counseling for you from the beginning."

"I had to make my own decision in my own way," Chidera says. "I had some rough spots. I'll probably have more." He looks at Miyanda. "But I have some help now."

Helena says, "I've taught you as much as I know. I have faith in you both." Helena embraces Chidera, then Miyanda. "I may see you in a few months."

Chidera feels a familiar low rumble beneath his feet. The doorway rises, revealing the maglev. A final wave, and Helena boards the train.

Chidera squeezes Miyanda's hand. "Ready?" he asks.

"I think so. Helena said it. Living in paradise isn't for the weak. Take away the need to work. Take away the abuse. The humiliation. You find out who you really are."

Chidera says, "I think we're both exactly who we need to be right now."

The maglev rumbles away. Chidera and Miyanda, arm in arm, stride toward their new life.

Kayonga's Decision

When I needed a character faced with the moral dilemma portrayed in this story, I immediately thought of Kayonga Tedesco from "Beyond Human Measure," since he had seen how Carrie Molina coped with a crushing decision in that story. Later in this collection, you'll see him cope with another hard choice in the story "A Grand Gesture." It seems moral dilemmas are part of the format for Kayonga's stories.

———

Why does that mass of stars seem to be reaching out to me? Kayonga Tedesco wondered as he floated within the clear viewing bubble of the starcraft *Belyanka*. With the lights out and giant Jupiter on the opposite side of the ship, the full glory of the stars shone before him, and one particularly large grouping of those points of fire appeared to him as misshapen arms advancing toward him. *My own personal constellation*, he thought.

Kayonga knew this was an illusion borne of a restless mind searching for patterns as he waited for the priest to arrive. All the same, he accepted the image as a comfort, something he'd found in short supply in recent days.

The viewing bubble's door slid aside and the priest floated in, pushing off against the edge of the doorway with a practiced ease. He landed next to Kayonga and offered his hand to shake. "Father Dominic Clarkson."

"Kayonga Tedesco."

Father Dominic indicated the starfield beyond the clear walls. "Beautiful, isn't it?"

Kayonga decided not to share his impression of the stars reaching out for him. "Almost beyond Human understanding, I'd say."

"I believe it takes us back to our most primitive days. When all the stars were *above* us, not all around."

"That makes sense to me. Uh . . . how do I go about this?"

"Typically, a Catholic says, 'Forgive me, Father, for I have sinned.' And you tell me how long it's been since your last confession."

"I'm not Catholic."

"Oh. Well, as ship's chaplain, I can do any number of flavors."

"I've described myself as a sect of one. And we were just looking out at its scriptures."

"I think I understand," Father Dominic said. "Then let me just ask how I can help you."

"I'm scheduled to leave on this ship, to become an explorer. But I'm uncertain as to whether I should."

"What's caused that uncertainty?"

"Haven't you heard of my actions, Father? Don't you know why I come to you so ashamed?"

"Never mind what I've heard. I want to hear your story as you need to tell it."

"Very well, Father."

———

It involved a rescue attempt gone awry deep in Jupiter's atmosphere (Kayonga told Father Dominic), and it threatened to become a double disaster. And I found myself the only person in a position to bring help in time.

It meant running to the only shuttle on Callisto Base that could get fired up and ready to go in time, and even then bypassing a dozen safety protocols and pre-flight procedures. Not to mention leaving without a co-pilot, which was strictly against protocol. But I had to lift as quickly as possible from that moon's dark, pock-marked surface.

Once I had the gravitic drive straining to erase the distance between Callisto and Jupiter, I got on the comm to my friend Michael Pearson, and found myself fighting to keep my voice steady and professional, not letting the fear I felt for him leak through: "What's your shuttle's status?"

Michael's response came back through a background of static: "Drive's out. We're sinking slowly so far, but sinking all the same. We've got no chance of making it on our own."

Michael and his co-pilot, Donna Gage, had launched earlier on a mission to help five Jupiter whales, three of them seriously injured.

Humans from Callisto Base had been communicating with the whales for several years, and Michael and Donna responded immediately to their call for help, only to find themselves traveling through a series of thunderheads nearly fifty kilometers tall that was generating lightning far stronger than any storms on Earth.

They took the risk.

And a bolt ten times as hot as the surface of the sun struck their shuttle, knocking out most of its systems. The craft immediately began to sink into the depths of Jupiter's atmosphere. Soon the pressure there would crush the shuttle. It was slim consolation that it would only take a fraction of a second, too short a time for the Human nervous system to perceive it or feel any pain.

"What about the whales?" I asked as Jupiter loomed ahead, with some of its yellow, red, and brown bands of clouds as wide as six hundred kilometers. I was guiding the craft to an area of the giant planet several hundred kilometers north of the Great Red Spot, which was a storm as wide as Earth itself.

Michael said, "They're having a tough time of it. Two of them trying to lift three others — they're all getting pretty tired."

Adult Jupiter whales could grow to be half an kilometer long. Their bodies were filled with helium and heavier gases, allowing them to glide within the depths of the gas giant's atmosphere.

Three of them had flown down into calmer skies where they fed on much smaller lifeforms. One of them, however, a youngster, strayed from the calm and wandered into an area where winds topped out at just over 360 kilometers an hour. The young whale's body couldn't take the buffeting, and two of the adults also ventured into the high wind area to rescue him. They were injured, in turn, and two more adults also risked their lives extracting all three of the stricken whales.

Now the two uninjured Jupiter whales were trying to bring the three injured ones up to calmer climes. They'd hoped Michael's shuttle could use its enticement beams to help lift them, but now that craft needed rescue, as well.

"How much time do you have left?" I asked.

Michael's voice was unsteady as he said, "About eight minutes until enough systems break down that we're crushed."

I measured his speed against the distance he had to cover. "I can just make it."

Another voice came over the datalink: "This is the Human Kayonga Tedesco?"

One of the Jupiter whales, I realized. "Yes, it is."

"This is Entai, the mother of my pod. We are all weakening. We will fall into the world before your shuttle does. I fear all of us will die."

Another quick check of speed and distance, and I said, "I can't bring you up and the Human craft as well."

"I am looking out for my pod. I will sacrifice myself if you can save the other four of us, then the Humans."

I shook my head. "I still wouldn't be able to save both them and the Human shuttle. Michael, are you *sure* of that timeline?"

"Just seven minutes now," Michael said. "Are you headed this way?"

A chill went through my body. "I . . . gotta decide!"

"*Decide*? Com'on, man, your mom's like an extra parent to me. What would she say?"

I realized exactly what she would say, as memories welled up:

My mother letting me decide, at age seven, whether to "tell" on another boy who'd stolen a ring from one of her friends. I told, even though I knew some of my friends would shun me.

Age fourteen, taking on a 17-year-old who'd knocked a young boy to the ground. I took a pounding, but the 17-year-old left the younger boy alone after that.

Michael's voice was back in my ear: "Kayonga, we're friends! Donna's got sisters, nieces back home! You can't be considering — "

"That's a whole family of whales — there's . . . there's . . . "

"Just two of us? I don't like putting it like this, but —

90

Donna and I, we're, you know."

Human, I thought.

Entai's voice broke in again. "As someone who is a different species from you, I understand if you save the Humans. But as a mother, I ask you to save my youngest, Itrak, and my other children Lilyn, Therach, and Serild."

I made my decision. I set the shuttle on a new course. "Michael — Donna — I'm sorry."

"Goddam it, Kayonga! How can you do this? I — I loved you!"

As I neared the Jupiter whales and activated the shuttle's enticement beam, all I could say was, "You had it right. About what my mother would say."

I remembered my mother praising me, hugging me after I revealed the identity of the thieving child, remembered her telling me how proud of me she was as she treated my cuts and bruises from the bully's beating.

And as my shuttle approached the whales and its enticement beam drew them upwards toward safety, as I wished I could press my hands against my ears to shut out Michael's final, screaming protests, I remembered just what she told me each time: "You can usually tell the right choice to make," she said. "It's the one that hurts the most."

———

As he finished his story, Kayonga floated with his eyes tightly closed against the brilliance of the stars. Father Dominic said, "Do you really believe that?"

Kayonga looked at the priest. "I don't know what to believe, Father. In the last few days I've been called a murderer. A traitor to my own race. Why would God test me in such a way?"

"The eternal question. All religions must try to answer it at some point. I'm partial to one of the Psalms -- 'Your word is a lamp to my feet and a light to my path.'"

Kayonga rubbed his eyes. "That doesn't seem to provide an answer, Father. Just comfort. And I'm not a Christian."

"All right, then. Other flavors. The Quran says, 'No calamity befalls on the earth or in yourselves but is inscribed in the Book of Decrees before We bring it into existence.'"

"So the pen writes, and we're helpless before it? That's not even a comfort."

"All right. The Buddha taught that we suffer because we desire something."

"Is desiring not to be thought of as a murderer so wrong?"

"I'm running out of flavors, Kayonga. One of my dearest friends is an atheist. Sometimes I think he sums it up perfectly."

"How's that?"

"Shit happens."

Kayonga smiled. "If only it were that simple. Maybe I should take heart from an explorer from several decades ago. Alexander Barron -- you know the name?"

"Of course. Made his reputation out here in Jupiter space. Flew the first missions into its atmosphere."

"He once said, 'I've never believed in God; but I believe in Creation.'" Kayonga aimed his gaze toward the stars again. "I believe I understand what he meant. The very idea of God mystifies me now."

Father Dominic said, "But you see His works before you."

"And that guides my decision," Kayonga said. "I'll become an explorer. I'll head out among the stars." He pressed his hand against the surface of the bubble, as if he could touch that mass of light that appeared to be reaching toward him. "They, at least, are willing to reveal themselves to me."

Shepherding

What if a beautiful natural phenomenon was also a threat to your homeworld's ecology? That idea was the spark for this story, as well as the opportunity to do some interesting world-building detailing the nature of the planet Seura and its native lifeforms.

———

As Eric Barre accompanied his wife and children down to New Laitila's small dock at the edge of the Surrette River, their herds of merra and doxar following, he searched his consciousness for the emotions he knew he should be feeling -- an impending sense of loss at their departure for their southern residence in Springhaven, regret that he'd spent so little time with them these past few months, concern that Sofia must take care of the children and manage their livestock all alone.

All those feelings, however, were subsumed beneath

swirling images of Seura's ring system, that swarm of fragments of stone and metal, some as large as houses, others mere specks of dust, all part of his effort to find a solution to an ecological crisis.

Eric zipped his jacket against the unseasonably cold breeze. He gazed toward the western sky, where the narrowing bands of the rings were backlit by the setting sun, and their edges glowed silvery, yellow, red, or purple depending upon how the sun's light shone upon them. He moved his gaze to the southern horizon, where the rings formed a celestial arch of intricate beauty, one that religiously-minded Humans had compared to a gateway into heaven. That arch provided both constancy and variety to Seura's skies -- constancy by the mere fact of their unyielding presence, variety in that they appeared different every time you gazed upon them.

Normally, Eric could never dispute their beauty, but given his current mental focus, the more closely he looked, the more he focused on objective detail: rings within rings within rings, and patterns within them that formed spokes, braids, and ringlets.

As he stood on the dock next to Sofia, however, Eric moved his focus to Sofia's features.

What he saw: her furrowed brow, clenched jaw muscles, her hand running nervously across her bald head. Her unblinking eyes aimed at him as if straining to understand who this man had become.

Eric pointed upstream. "Look," he told Sofia. "The tempaq." The living cargo boat had just come into sight. It was fifty meters long and ten meters wide.

Eric and Sofia gathered the sheaths of yellowish-green, thick, and spongy grass that would coax the boat to shore and nourish it during Sofia's trip southward. If the Humans had not been at the dock providing the grasses it desired, it would've returned upstream to its usual feeding and nesting areas.

The tempaq's wide flat deck narrowed toward the bow into a torso and head about the size of a walrus, with similar fatty folds. The tempaq's expression implied dignity and a hint of sadness -- loose folds of skin surrounded surprisingly small, rheumy eyes. Small withered arms jutted from its chest.

Sofia went to the river's edge and, waving the sheaths of grass, coaxed the tempaq closer to the shoreline. Its arms grasped the wood of the dock as it pulled itself into position at dockside. Sofia and Eric placed sheaths of the thick grass before the tempaq's eager mouth. Its feeding sounds were loud and enthusiastic.

Sofia looked upslope, clapped her hands twice, and the herds started toward the tempaq.

The dozen merra came first. They stood upright, most over two meters, and had a chest girth the size of horses. Their intelligence was comparable to Human children, and they were capable of simple speech. "One side, please," the lead merra, its voice a low growl, said to Eric as it eased past. The soft pads of its paws pounded dully against the ground as it trotted down the slope and onto the living boat.

Behind the merra came three doxar. Their long fur ranged from a burnt umber color to a blondish-red. They were beasts of burden, towing several large sledges behind them. The first sledge carried Sofia and Eric's children, 11-year-old Martin and 10-year-old Cacambo, along with their two girls, 8-year old Cunégonde and 7-year-old Paquette, who waved enthusiastically at their mom and dad, as if they were on parade. A part of Eric deep down in his consciousness wondered how long their enthusiasm would last, if they'd soon realize they weren't coming home anytime soon, if ever.

The final two sledges carried bundles of spices, vegetables, and various tech units. Behind the sledges was a cloud of insects, some natural, others synthetic. On a farm, the merra grew and harvested the crops, and the doxar provided milk and transport. The natural insects pollinated new crops and the synthetic ones herded the natural ones and monitored for plant diseases or blights. Sofia often joked that it was all the fun of farming without most of the work.

Sofia and Eric remained on the dock as all their creatures boarded the tempaq. The animals and the children shuffled for position on its broad deck. Eric was vaguely gratified to see Sofia chuckle as the merra tried to impose order upon the chaos and failed. The children, in particular, were singularly successful at eluding the merra among the many loose folds of deck skin.

"I wish you wouldn't go," Eric said. "I might have the problem solved in a few days."

"If it doesn't work, though, we'll be late getting to our southern home."

"It'll work."

Sofia faced Eric. She raised her hand toward his face, hesitated just a moment, then ran her fingers down the side of his face and neck.

To Eric, it felt as if she were rubbing his face with gravel. He pulled her hand away.

Sofia said, "I only meant -- "

As she spoke, Sofia's words faded into the background for Eric as his thoughts encompassed a waking dream of ring shadow that kept some of the most fertile areas of Seura in darkness half the year.

Sofia ended, " -- I want my husband back."

Eric shook his head to help himself emerge from his waking dream. "I'm . . . sorry. What was that?"

"I *said*, as much as I want you to solve the problem of the rings, I want *you* -- I want my husband back. I'm fearful of what you've made yourself into."

Eric took Sofia's hands, and this time he felt the warmth, the softness, of her flesh. For this moment, could relate to her as a loved one, and not a distraction. "I'm sorry. It's how I have to be to . . . "

"To get the job done. I know. *Please* be successful. We can make a life together even coping with the rings. We can't if you're going to ignore us in favor of the rings. If you're going to show these flashes of anger."

"The anger," Eric said, "is what motivates me. It gives me focus."

Sofia didn't say anything more. She embraced Eric and he held onto his humanity long enough for his embrace to be genuinely affectionate.

Sofia boarded the tempaq, which began its sluggish journey downriver toward Springhaven. That trip would take a couple of days.

With the sun close on the horizon, shadow began to obscure the rings' eastern arc. In turn, the darkened portion of the rings blocked the view of that part of the sky. Even so, the rest of the arch shone so brightly that only the most brilliant stars remained visible.

Eric stood on the dock until the veiled sun sank below the horizon, darkening Seura's rings, making them an ethereal presence in the moonless sky.

———

As he headed back toward their farm at the edge of the town of New Laitila, Eric considered the task he would face the next day.

Seura's rings weren't quite two centuries old, having

formed when the planet's only moon entered the planet's Roche Limit and shattered. That was recently enough in astronomical terms that the rings were only now upsetting the planet's ecological balance in the areas where their broad shadows fell. They'd affected the life cycles of everything from the ubiquitous strandwood trees and fingermoss to Seuran animals such as the wildtooth and doxar.

Many animals were changing migratory and breeding habits. Merra were having more offspring than was usual, only to see fewer of them live to maturity. Doxar in some cases refused to breed at all, and even mature ones were finding it more difficult to gain nourishment from the plant species remaining.

Such ring systems had always fascinated Eric and he'd wanted to study one up close. Sofia had always wanted to live on a farm. They'd come to Seura expecting it to be a place they could both live out their dreams.

But now Eric faced a task he'd never anticipated; he had to modify the rings, perhaps destroy them to save Seura's ecological balance.

Once he returned home, Eric was barely aware of fixing himself a light supper of a salad, and washing it down with some iced tea. Most of his consciousness concerned itself with the mechanics of molding Seura's rings into a form that would allow more sunlight onto the planet's surface.

I'm afraid my approach is going to be needlessly sudden, even violent, Eric thought. *But we don't have time for a more subtle, long-term solution.*

Seura's rings had no effect in the summer on the northern hemisphere, where New Laitila, and their farm, was located. Then, the planet's axial tilt meant its primary's rays cast "over" the rings. Or, to look at it from the planetary viewpoint, the sun was high in the skies, and the rings didn't eclipse it.

Winter was a different matter. Then the rings did eclipse the sun's rays in the northern hemisphere. That made winters even colder and darker than they would be otherwise.

The rings were ephemeral, though: over the next few thousand years, the ring system would break up on its own.

Humanity couldn't wait that long.

With his meal finished, Eric made his way to his bedroom. *Our* bedroom, he reminded himself as the visualizations of Seura's ring system arose again, soon to take over his entire consciousness, to force thoughts of Sofia and his children into the background.

This was my decision, he thought, *mine alone, to allow biotech into my body to allow me to focus so completely on my visualizations, to go beyond mere calculations any computer could make, and into the conceptual imaging allowing me to conceive new, more benign patterns for the rings.*

Lying in bed, though, Eric's emotions managed to well up for a brief moment, forcing him to relive recent incidents he'd rather forget:

-- Grabbing Paquette's arm in anger as she interrupted his studies of the rings one afternoon, and barely noticing her jagged cries as Sofia took her to another room to comfort her.

-- Sofia recoiling from him during an argument about the ring project as he stood, eyes tightly closed, fists clenched. He never took a step toward her, but in a more lucid moment, he realized he'd never seen her so frightened, and never dreamed that he'd ever be the reason for that fright.

But those concerns faded as that same biotech sent his awareness flying among the spokes and braids of the intricate patterns of the rings in the moments before sleep took him.

———

Early the next morning, a shuttlecraft took Eric up to the Unity archeological starcraft *Kathleen Kenyon*. He barely spoke to the two crewmembers on board, as images of Seura's ring system dominated the outside view.

The *Kenyon*, given its exploratory mission, was a relatively small ship. Its commander, Andrea Boca, was a woman who looked as if she was in her thirties, except for her eyes. *They don't actually make her look older,* Eric realized. *Just wiser. Something rejuv treatments can't hide. Not that you'd want them to.*

Those eyes looked at him with a piercing gaze, and Eric wondered why for an instant until he realized his own expression must be distracted at best. "Sorry if I seem a little distant, Captain," he said. He indicated the main bridge viewscreen, which showed a closeup of the arc of Seura's rings, with the planet in the background. "You might say, I'm more out there among the rings than I am here on your bridge."

"We'll hope that's for the best, then," Captain Boca said. She introduced Eric to Ensign Yuri Vasilev, the ship's chief weapons officer. Here on this archeological ship, the weapons were rather basic and normally used only for defense.

Vasilev told Eric, "We don't get much of a chance to fire these things except in practice."

Capt. Boca said, "Yuri, don't be too modest." She turned to Eric. "He's the best at what he does. If he weren't, I'd never allow this, given the concerns I already have about this project. One shot, and fragments of ring material the size of a house could get thrown from orbit and strike the planet."

Eric said, "I've allowed for that in my calculations. And at the first sign of any danger, we stop down."

"I find that reassuring," Capt. Boca said in a tone of voice that implied she did not.

Eric told Vasilev, "I'll need to work right beside you. I'll be providing your targets."

Vasilev took Eric to a console on one side of the bridge. "It's all set up," he said. "Cube imaging of the rings, interface with the weapons. You say you want a particular part of the rings gone, it's gone."

The solution Eric had come up with was to destroy as many shepherd moons within the rings as possible. The gravity of such moons maintained a planetary ring's sharp edges, keeping the ring stable.

First, the *Kenyon's* enticement beams would grab hold of a selected shepherd moon, moving it from its position within the rings. Then disruptors would turn them into fine dust. That, in turn, was supposed to allow the Seuran rings to spread out sufficiently that they would allow more sunlight onto the planet's surface -- a quick, violent solution to a long-term, subtle ecological change.

Eric fought to balance Vasilev's words alongside the images of the rings within his mind as he said, "We'd better get started."

A display grid appeared on the main viewscreen, overlaying real-time pictures of the ring system. Vasilev worked the *Kenyon's* weapons console with a sure touch, setting up a firing pattern. He turned toward Captain Boca: "We're ready, Captain."

Captain Boca told the weapons tech, "If the smallest fragment goes wild, you know what to do."

"Aye, ma'am," Vasilev said. "The mission becomes how to destroy or at least divert that fragment."

After another moment's hesitation, Captain Boca said, "Fire when ready."

Eric worked the console in front of him, the small cube display of the ring system overlaid now with the comp's calculations informed by his insights into how to mold the rings into a less destructive form.

Eric highlighted one of the nearest shepherd moons, a moonlet several kilometers across whose gravitational pull was barely strong enough to hold close the gaps among the smaller ring fragments surrounding it. Otherwise, those fragments would drift apart. Multiply that effect over the entire expanse of the rings, and wider, more diffuse rings would form.

At least that was the plan. "There's your target," he said.

Vasilev pressed the firing control. The silent beam was invisible in the vacuum of space until it reached the edge of the ring, then Eric saw it as a thread of light that struck the center of the targeted shepherd.

The cube image Eric was watching bloomed into an image of pure white light for an instant. When that light faded, all that was left of the moonlet were more ring particles expanding outward in a wave that encompassed the main body of the rings for half a kilometer or more.

"Great job!" he told Vasilev. *Well, that part worked,* Eric thought. *But that's the easy part. The hard part is doing it again and again and seeing if it makes a difference.*

All the same, the necessity for this destruction saddened him. His primary motivation was to rid Seura of the ecological effects of its ring system. What had originally brought him to Seura, however, was an eagerness to discover more about the rings. It was unfortunate in a way, even regarding lifeless rock, but you learned a lot about something by destroying it. The part of Eric's consciousness that was concentrated on the rings themselves eagerly absorbed details of the moonlet's structure, its tensile strength, whether it contained water -- all the information its destruction revealed.

Eric provided Vasilev with another target, then another. Despite his misgivings, the work exhilarated him as he watched entire sections of the rings already spreading out, becoming more diffuse.

Even as Eric kept targeting more shepherd moons, he examined the consequences of his work. Exactly how much more sunlight would make its way down to the shadowed portions of the planet? Even though the changes in the rings had just begun, the comp could extrapolate the endgame from these preliminary results.

The shock of the initial conclusions made all of Eric's concentration on the ring patterns fall away.

The rings wouldn't become diffuse enough. Yes, more sunlight would reach the ground, but it wouldn't be sufficient to restore Seura's ecological balance.

Eric pounded his fist on the console before him. He barely heard Capt. Boca telling Vasilev to cease fire.

———

Back in his empty house on Seura, Eric had never felt so alone. Sofia was gone, the children were gone, and as he moved through the house he could hear every creak of every floorboard, every gust of wind as it whistled within the ceiling or inside the walls, every drip of water from the kitchen faucet.

He made himself a cup of coffee and sat at the kitchen table, trying to decide what to do next.

Capt. Boca was pissed at him, first for screwing up the project, second for insisting upon returning planetside to his home, necessitating another shuttle trip. No doubt she'd be pissed a third time if he insisted upon coming back up to the *Kenyon*.

If I go back up at all, he thought.

Eric forced down the now-useless images of the ring system that tried to impinge upon his consciousness again. *Where did I go wrong? I wanted so badly to help my planet, to help everyone on it. I became angry, I wanted to lash out against the rings themselves.*

Sudden realization: *That's the problem. I wanted to strike out. I was angry at the rings, angry at nature itself for creating them and threatening the world that has become my home.*

Eric stood as a new series of visualizations appeared in his mind. Now he knew how to tackle the problem of the rings and make it work.

I've got to get hold of Capt. Boca, he thought. *Whether she's pissed or not, I know this new method will work. I know it will.*

But an instant of reflection made him stand in the middle of his kitchen with his hands pressing against the sides of his head, his eyes squeezed shut. *I know these visualizations are taking me over again. But I've got to keep a part of myself free, got to remain aware of what really counts -- Sofia, Martin, Cacambo, Cunégonde, and Paquette.*

———

The next day found Eric back on board the *Kathleen Kenyon*. Capt. Boca's attitude toward him as she stared at him from her commander's chair was professional but reserved. Ensign Vasilev seemed more skeptical than he had the day before, but Eric couldn't concern himself with that as long as the man did his job.

Today, though, Vasilev wasn't at the weapons position.

He'd be operating the enticement beam projector himself -- pushing here, pulling there, using the patterns of force at his disposal to mold the rings rather than carve on them.

The *Kenyon* was closing in on the outer edge of the rings, and once again Eric was impressed at their complexity as he leaned forward to better see the patterns of braids and ringlets and spokes on the cube projection.

Captain Boca told Eric, "I want to hear directly from you exactly how all this works."

Eric explained, "The key is to move individual moonlets and make them into shepherd moons. It's all how you place them among the various rings that make up the total ring system. You need one between the individual ring and Seura, and the other out beyond the ring, and you do that with as many of the individual rings as possible."

Capt. Boca asked, "To what end?"

"Narrowing the larger ring system. Every such system has gaps between its rings, and shepherd moons can create those gaps. Move the shepherds into different positions, then we can fill those gaps and create a narrower set of rings. Given the planet's axial tilt, the areas that had been in shadow will take turns getting more sunlight."

"So rather than a more diffuse ring system, we'll have a narrower one, and more sunlight will still get through to the planet's surface."

"That's exactly right."

Capt. Boca didn't say anything more. A nod and a wave of her hand were enough for Eric to begin the process. Within moments, *Kenyon's* enticement beams were focused on an unaccompanied moonlet. A computer simulation -- and Eric's best intuition -- had picked it as the best candidate to make into a shepherd moon elsewhere in the ring system.

After a time, Capt. Boca spoke up: "How long will it take to transport that moonlet where we need it to go?"

Eric stared at the cube readout. "One of the requirements I have for picking shepherd moons is that we won't have to take them far. This one has to go about a thousand K, in the direction of the rings' rotation. It ought to take about half a day."

"And the whole process?"

Eric faced the captain. "We should know within a few days whether Sofia and the kids can come back home."

"That quickly?"

"The rings won't have been altered that quickly. But we'll see the trend by then. We'll know if this is going to work."

———

Two weeks later. Eric and Sofia stood behind their home, where Martin, Cacambo, Cunégonde, and Paquette, exhausted from their brief jaunt down much of the Surrette River and back again, were already in bed. The doxar were back in their accustomed fields, with the merra, docile as ever, watching over them.

Eric felt Sofia's fingertips touching the palm of his hand. He took her hand in his. *A small forgiveness*, he thought. *Maybe something bigger can grow from it.*

Eric pointed toward the rings, which were visible only as a shadowy presence in the night sky. "See? We used to stand here and the western arch of the ring would be this huge arch over that ridge over there. Now it disappears behind it. The rings will adjust even more as the new shepherds continue to draw ring material toward themselves."

"Such a quick change," Sofia said. "And it means we can live where we want. I'd given up hope, and I apologize for that. I didn't have enough confidence in you."

"I have a lot more to apologize for. The way I let my anger take control. I frightened you. I'm sure when I made Paquette cry, I frightened all the children."

"You needed that anger, you said."

"I was a goddam liar, and didn't even know it. But all that's fading now. I had the biotech taken out. No more waking dreams about spokes and braids and ringlets. Now it's just us and the children, as it's supposed to be."

The rings were a dark, starless presence in Seuran skies as Sofia stepped into Eric's embrace.

Silhouettes

This is the fourth story I've published about my series character Leo Bakri. The previous stories, "The Human Equations," "Unbound," and "The Unfinished Man," all appeared in my earlier collection THE HUMAN EQUATIONS. It was there that I explained how "The Human Equations" was written in the first person, and that I forgot that when I wrote "Unbound" in the third person.

By the time of "The Unfinished Man," however, I was very aware of that and decided to tell that third Leo Bakri story from the viewpoint of another of my series characters, Mike Christopher. So when I approached "Silhouettes," I knew I had to keep the concept going. More details forthcoming in the afterword.

TRANSMISSION #1109 from Leo Bakri, planet Keleni, received 05/29/2151

at Exobiology Center, Newton Habitat University:

SCIENCE REPORT #308
GLIDING INTO PARENTHOOD

PERSONAL NOTE:

Yes, I'm well aware of the disdain the "colorful" portions of my titles, along with my informal style, bring among some humorless individuals within the scientific community. To which I say, tough shit. This may be my last major scientific report from the planet Keleni, so I'll title it as I wish. All right, let's pretend it has a subtitle: "An Examination of Birth Patterns Among Manta Gliders of the planet Keleni," how's that?

I'm also attaching excerpts from my personal notes to this report, since I'm told that my "adventures" make good copy in the university's newsletters. Conflicting messages, anyone?

I suppose the university can't help it, though, if people are fascinated to learn what kind of trouble a man of 87 years (which isn't that old!) who has to use an exoskeleton to get around has gotten himself into now.

Ugh. Even with the exoskeleton I'm pretty tired even before I start out. Not having a good day. But I can't let myself dwell on that. I didn't bring myself all these light-years from Earth just to sit around.

SCIENCE REPORT (CONT.):

On Day One of my little expedition, I started out in my squat, armored rover, leaving my small home, which huddles close to the ground to protect itself from the planet's eternal windstorms and hurricanes. The trip would only be a quick flight in my shuttle, but the rover contains the better set of research equipment and is slightly more comfortable if I end up spending a few days at the remote site.

ATTACHMENT: Details of Keleni ecology:

Keleni spins three times faster than Earth, with stronger winds, possibly up to 100 to 200 kph, and more violent hurricanes and other storms, larger waves, and more lightning. It has more jet streams, more turbulence. Hurricanes can last for weeks or months . . . .

PERSONAL NOTE:

Even encased within the rover, it feels as if Keleni is trying to scour me off its surface. The vehicle shakes and rocks back and forth, making driving that much more difficult, especially since I've already been feeling tired all day.

Living here the past few years, though, has allowed me to view many marvels, such as what I call the Great White Spot, a massive hurricane twelve years old that hovers over this world's largest ocean, never trying to sneak toward land. But those "normal" 200-kph winds over land areas have brought wonder enough, given how they've forced animals such as the manta glider to adapt.

SCIENCE REPORT (CONT.):

The rover made the usual slow progress across Keleni's landscape, which of course has no roads to aid its advance. On Earth, one might follow common pathways of animals through thick vegetation or woodland areas, but this world's constant tempests erase such paths as quickly as they're formed.

At one point, as the rover made its way through a shallow valley, the winds whipped up so severely I raised the vehicle's six wide wheels to let it settle onto the ground. I deployed the support claws to grasp the earth and keep the rover from being blown away, and me along with it. I registered peak winds of 350 kph!

After about ten minutes, those winds slacked off just enough for me to retract the claws, lower the wheels, and get the hell out of that valley.

Given its rapid rotation, a day on Keleni is only eight hours long. I'd started my journey at sunrise, but only four hours later I hadn't yet reached my destination and with the sun setting, I decided to wait to proceed any farther.

PERSONAL NOTE:

Given my own physical limitations, my preference is to wait out the night, no matter how many lights, night vision devices, and lifeform sensors I may have. I'm at the mercy of my technology and how it interacts with this violent planet, and I prefer not to push its limits, especially on days when I'm feeling tired even before I start a particular project.

SCIENCE REPORT (CONT.):

Eight hours after I began, it was now Day Two of my expedition. Within about an hour and a half, I arrived at the manta gliders' breeding grounds. I deployed the rover's claws again, purely as a precaution. I made the usual checks on my exoskeleton and left the rover.

Winds were light for Keleni -- about 75 kph. With the sun

climbing into the sky so quickly, if you stood in one spot and watched your shadow, you could see it growing shorter and stouter from one moment to the next. The landscape was dominated by plants I'd dubbed sunnysiders, which featured red and blue cylindrical leaves that tracked the sun throughout the short day. Their wide roots anchored them firmly into the soil against even the strongest winds.

Some of the manta gliders concealed themselves among the sunnysiders. Still more gliders hid among groups of other animals called daggerheads, which resembled manta gliders from above. The gliders were taking advantage of the fact that daggerheads weren't tasty to many flying predators, essentially saying, "See, I'm not tasty either!"

My exoskeleton held me unmoving at the side of the rover as I deployed a low-slung equipment module that lowered itself from the rear of the rover and walked itself to the edge of the manta gliders' breeding grounds. It opened up, its metal flaps sliding closely along its skin to keep the winds from catching them and blowing the module over.

Various components slid, rolled, or flew from the module. Most would, in turn, launch nanite probes that would seek out the slumbering manta gliders in their caves or shallow holes, burrow into the ground, or take flight. They would record cubes and flat images of the gliders and their prey, as well as the creatures who, in turn, preyed upon the gliders.

ATTACHMENT: Details of manta gliders:

The animals use tens of thousands of tiny legs working in concert, almost like flagella on sea creatures. Those legs allow the manta glider to move with incredible grace and agility. Its "wings," anywhere from half a meter to two meters wide, can glide over virtually any surface. Sometimes the manta glider literally glides, tilting itself so that flowing air pushes against its underside to lift it and propel it along.

The manta glider feeds mostly on insects, but they're especially fond of small sedentary animals called nesters. They can sting a nester with a poison that immobilizes it. The manta glider then takes it slowly into its body and digests it over a period of days. This eliminates the need for feeding for awhile, but also makes the manta glider vulnerable to other predators during that time.

The gestation period of the manta gliders is about two months, and the mother will only feed a couple of times, hiding in a cave or hole the rest of the time to protect itself from predators such as mud walkers and wind sprinters, which are faster and stronger than they are . . . .

PERSONAL NOTE:

So -- have you noticed that undercurrent of dissatisfaction or cynicism in parts of my little report here? Gentle bitching about "disdain" or downplaying my "adventures," and making sure to mention my exoskeleton -- something a man in early middle age like myself should never have needed if I'd gone ahead and had rejuv when I was supposed to.

Don't worry, it's nothing the university or anyone else has done. If I feel as if I'm a damaged soul, it's all of my own doing.

Listen to me -- "damaged soul," indeed. What a bunch of pretentious crap. The truth is, I'm not certain whether I want to go on living much longer.

Oh, not for me the lamenting and the ennui and pointing a disruptor at my head. It's just that it's taken me this many decades do realize the reason I neglected my own health was because I didn't feel I was worthy of living longer.

But let's set the melodrama aside for now, shall we?

SCIENCE REPORT (CONT.):

With the winds fairly calm, at least by Keleni standards, many of the pregnant manta gliders were out in the open. I saw a few who had already enveloped nesters and were heading into the digestive phase. One hapless glider, in turn, was being stalked by a mud walker. Imagine a furry, egg-shaped being with stubby legs. You couldn't underestimate its speed, however. Those little legs soon overtook the food-burdened manta glider and pounced upon it. It was a slow-motion pouncing, though, given that the mud walker was about half the size of the manta glider and still had to stay as close to the ground as possible even on a calm day.

Manta gliders breathe through trachea situated on their backs. The mud walker pressed itself against that trachea until the glider suffocated. Then it fed upon the glider. If enough of the nester the glider had been feeding on was left, it would consume that, as well.

By the time the mud walker had its fill, the sun was setting yet again. From my vantage point just outside the rover, I could barely make out its silhouette as it left behind the remains of the manta glider and the nester. Its outline faded away as it entered a stand of sunnysiders which had turned themselves to soak in those last remaining bits of sunlight.

PERSONAL NOTE:

Yeah, sometimes I feel as if I'm the one fading away here on Keleni. My exile has been self-imposed, but some days I feel no less destitute for all that. Some days I feel as if I'm the silhouette, and my real self is the one at the mercy of a source of illumination and being perceived from the proper angle.

Or maybe this is just a lot of bullshit that I'm thinking because I's so tired. Now I'm getting short of breath. I think I'd fall down if my exoskeleton wasn't holding me up.

Oh, crap, a medical alert!

MED ALERT, THROUGH DATALINK:

"This is a medical alert. Access diagnostic bed immediately. If unable, request help through datalink. Exoskeleton can also transport you."

PERSONAL NOTE:

OK, so maybe I have to embrace some of the melodrama after all. I was about to fall over, but at my command, my exoskeleton got me inside the rover and onto this bed. Its medical tech isn't as advanced as what I have back in my house, but it'll do for now.

Seems I'm having some kind of "event" relating to cardiomyopathy.

The bed has injected me with some medical nanites that are checking out my heart rate, blood pressure, how well I'm breathing, and my body's oxygen saturation.

After the fact, I realized I was getting short of breath even as I deployed the equipment module. Now it's tough for me even to lie down on the bed. Turns out that's a symptom, too.

The solution? Turns out there's a list. ACE inhibitors. Beta blockers. Heart pacemaker. Heart transplant, or, in my case, an artificial implant, since I don't think a manta glider or mud walker would be a suitable donor.

But remember the part where I wasn't worthy of a long life?

SCIENCE REPORT (CONT.):

Work continued in my absence as the countless nanite probes began to report back. They revealed details of the physiological changes the manta gliders went through during their pregnancies, and how they used various tactics to keep from becoming prey, especially in the latter stages of gestation. And in just a few days or even hours, they should start giving birth, some of them away in their hidey-holes, others right out in the open beneath 100-plus kph winds or higher.

ATTACHMENT: Survival strategies in manta gliders during pregnancy:

Given that pregnant manta gliders are generally abandoned by their mates after the conception of their child, the females of the species must engage in several strategies to survive . . . .

PERSONAL NOTE:

I really don't feel like going over any of that data right now. For my own sake, I really should get back to my house, where I have access to more and better medical tech. But that would mean abandoning this science mission, and this kind of thing is the whole reason I'm here on Keleni.

That, and the continuing effort to try to forget my past.

Oh, I could've had my memories snipped. But that's cheating. Just as, somewhere deep down, I've always thought having rejuv treatments was cheating. We live the time we're meant do.

Said the man hooked up to a diagnostic bed, brought there by an exoskeleton, his bloodstream teeming with medical nanotech.

What was that about a foolish consistency?

Decades ago, working in law enforcement, I took a man convicted of a simple assault charge aboard an orbital habitat down to Earth where he died in a terrorist attack. Blamed myself.

Served on a starcraft during the Great Human War and kept the engineering module's blast doors open enough during an attack that my lover Marie Sovel could get out. Endangered the ship in the process.

That, they made me forget. Marie was the love of my life, and they wiped away all knowledge of her as anything other than a co-worker. Punishment for my crime, though I found out later what had happened. Guess that's why I'm so leery of the snip now.

Then came years, decades, of study, after abandoning law enforcement and military duty and remaking myself as a scientist and explorer. I refrained from intimate human contacts of any sort, whether emotional or sexual. No time for tenderness or affection, plenty for applied planetology. Little time for meaningless sex, but lots for exobiology.

I've heard the idea that to embrace death is to accept it as part of life. But these manta gliders, while not sentient, don't accept that idea. They abandon the open spaces where they normally live for an underground existence as their children develop within them, coming out only when they can't deny their hunger any longer, emerging to track down prey even as they're at risk of becoming prey themselves.

They work, they fight, to live and to make sure their children live.

So I want to see how these manta gliders manage it, manage to give birth, with so much stacked against them.

But the biotech readings on this bed are telling me I may not last that long. In fact, they also tell me that heading back to my house for treatment may kill me, and even if I get there alive, any treatment is just prolonging the inevitable. Seems that all these years I've gone for the quick patch-up job, and now everything's coming loose at once.

So here's the next question -- what do I do now? Risk death for a chance to witness this miracle of birth, blah, blah, blah, as it happens? Or head back home to give myself a few more minutes or hours of life attached to more machines, simply pondering the events of my life as I have countless times over?

ATTACHMENT:

Automatic data upload from research nanites in absence of Human researcher.

Number of manta gliders examined: 136

Number who survived birth process: 107

Deaths of manta gliders and offspring due to complications with birth: 4.

Deaths of manta gliders and offspring due to predators: 25

PERSONAL LOG:

The moment I completed the above attachment, I was grateful that I decided to engage in what amounted to a celebration of new life rather than a consideration of the dead past. Considering the very existence of life is as close as I get to some sort of spirituality. I'd try to explain that, but it would probably just meet with more disdain for being too "colorful."

Tough shit. And don't bother begging for more.

This may be my last major scientific report from the planet Keleni. If it is, then just remember me as . . . .

TRANSMISSION #1109 from Leo Bakri, planet Keleni, ENDS.

TRANSMISSION #1110 from Bakri home A.I., planet Keleni, received 05/29/2151 at Exobiology Center, Newton Habitat University:

Leo Bakri lifesigns terminated. As per subject Bakri's request, his exoskeleton transported his remains outside the rover and atomized them. Approximate windspeed at moment of atomization: 215 kph.

TRANSMISSION #1110 from Bakri habitat A.I., planet Keleni, ENDS.

AFTERWORD

In this fourth outing with Leo Bakri, I wanted to tell the story from a point of view I hadn't used before, to continue the concept I'd sort of fallen into. With first-person, third-person, and telling a story from another character's POV already done, I wasn't left with a lot of options. I didn't feel up to trying second-person, which some readers resist, anyway, not liking being addressed as "you" the entire story, much like this: "You enter a room. Immediately, you see the intruder lunge at you, holding a knife."

So I thought I'd try an epistolary story, which usually is written as a series of letters or diary entries. This allowed me to have Leo tell his own story again as he would in a first-person story, while also allowing him to take a step back and relate background material quickly and efficiently in his science reports so I could avoid the dreaded "infodump."

I think it's clear this is the final Leo Bakri story, unless I come up with yet another way to tell one about him. Maybe an obituary or an encyclopedia article?

A Grand Gesture

Kayonga Tedesco returns! Having established in "Kayonga's Decision" that he was going to become an explorer, he seemed the natural character to place into this story, especially since he, reluctantly, specializes in moral dilemmas.

———

It's as if the very landscape is trying to keep us from making any head-way, Kayonga Tedesco thought. He and another crewmember, Amaia Moreau, trudged across a planetary surface covered with a tar-like substance. Their mission: a preliminary survey here on the carbon planet called Lucy to determine a proper location for a larger expedition.

But he felt like a man with two left feet trying to learn ballet. Each step he took amounted to a negotiation with the planet's surface -- lift one foot *this* much as the sticky landscape insisted upon pulling you back, lean forward *that* much while balancing in his protective lifesuit in grav that was one-third more intense than Earth's. Balance, always balance.

The entire time, he felt Amaia's eyes on him. Now he heard an exasperated sigh over his datalink. He tensed up even before Amaia spoke. He'd anticipated her impatience with him from the moment they'd been paired together on this mission. *I know you consider me too young and inexperienced,* he thought. Amaia, who was in her mid-fifties, was a couple decades older than Kayonga.

Behind them stood the shuttle, *Amur,* from the Earth Unity starcraft *Belyanka.* Kayonga felt they should've brought a third crewmember with them to stay aboard the shuttle in case of an emergency, but the *Belyanka's* commander, Gina Marianthal, overruled that decision, saying they'd never had a problem with two-person exploratory teams before.

Amaia told him, "We should've landed closer to that crater. There are plants just on this side of it I want to examine, especially since we might also find animal life near them."

Kayonga's shoulders slumped as he said, "We'll get to the plants in good time. And we didn't know if the land next to the crater would bear the shuttle's weight."

Amaia muttered, "Anything would be better than taking the chance of getting stuck like flies in amber."

I know there's another reason you dislike me, Kayonga thought. *But I can't allow myself to think about that now. Can't allow myself the distraction.*

Meanwhile, I'm surrounded by wonder and not taking any of it in! He and Amaia made their trek beneath thick clouds of carbon monoxide and carbon dioxide that blanketed Lucy's skies and seemingly dared its sun, Prudence, to show its face.

The plain before them led in the far distance to mountains mostly made of silicon carbides, the stuff Humans used to make ceramics. Beyond those mountains, Kayonga knew, was a broad sea of methane. But none of those was their immediate goal. That was a crater just a hundred meters distant.

Lined with diamond.

Diamond! The very word evoked thoughts of glamor and luxury, even though such baubles had little meaning against the backdrop of most Human societies anymore. Replicator technology could churn them out by the armful, and back in Earth system they were easily accessible within many asteroids that hoarded them within their interiors. They had little inherent value except in industrial uses.

Still, the glints of white fire that blazed from beyond the peaked rim of the crater, formed by the heat and pressure generated by a long-ago meteorite strike, drew Kayonga forward. The planet's name, Lucy, came from a reference to an old song involving diamonds, one Kayonga wasn't familiar with.

Soon the tarry landscape gave way to something resembling asphalt or coal. Within minutes, they arrived at the edge of the crater. Just enough of Prudence's rays pierced Lucy's smog-shrouded skies to set the crater glimmering with with countless glints of light. *It's as if it's beckoning to me,* Kayonga thought.

The bowl of the crater stood nearly a hundred meters across and about twenty deep. About twenty meters to their left stood a gentle rise, and, between that rise and the crater, a line of bright yellow vegetation. "I insist upon checking out the plants over there before we go down into the crater," Amaia said. Kayonga knew he was meant to hear the tone of barely contained exasperation in her voice.

Kayonga shook his head. "Listen, I'm tired of dealing with all this subtext any time you talk to me -- "

"Subtext?"

"That's right. I understand that this is more than resentment. You actually hate me. And it has nothing to do with where we landed the shuttle or how young I am."

Amaia held up a hand as if trying to ward off his next words. "Hate? That doesn't start to describe it. You offend me. You let a friend die!"

The moment of his decision thrust itself back into Kayonga's consciousness, its intensity undimmed across the weeks since he'd made it.

In Kayonga's previous posting, at Callisto Base orbiting Jupiter, he'd piloted a shuttle on a rescue mission deep in the giant planet's atmosphere. His friend Michael Pearson and Michael's co-pilot Donna Gage had started out on a rescue mission of their own to save five Jupiter whales. Three of the whales, whose bodies were filled with helium and other gases, had been injured while being buffeted in a storm with winds just over 360 kilometers an hour.

Michael and Donna were on the way to lift the whales to safety when a lightning bolt ten times as hot as the surface of the sun struck their shuttle, which began to sink into Jupiter's crushing atmosphere.

Kayonga found himself having to make a terrible decision. He had only enough time to save the two Humans or the five Jupiter whales.

He chose the larger number of beings. He chose the whales, even as his friend Michael pleaded with him, screamed at him in disbelief that a friend he loved was betraying him.

Kayonga left Callisto Base soon afterwards. He'd quickly tired of being called a murderer, a traitor to Humanity. He'd hoped to find some peace, or at least solace, out in space.

Thinking back on that now, though, a dark thought ran through Kayonga's consciousness: *The ideal explorer runs toward something, and I'm running away.*

To Amaia, though, she said, "I sacrificed two to save five."
"Your. Friend."

Kayonga bowed his head. "I know." He sat silently for a

moment, then said, "Do you want to go back up to *Belyanka?* I'm sure if you insist, Captain Marianthal will pair you with someone else. The two of us were just a tryout, anyway." *Maybe I should give up entirely,* Kayonga thought. *Just head back to Ghana. Sit on the beach, stare at the night skies, the stars.*

Kayonga saw, through the faceplate of Amaia's lifesuit, how she held her head high. "*No.* I take my assignments as given."

Kayonga didn't know whether to be frustrated or relieved. "Then lead the way," he said. As they continued onward, the voice of Kayonga's friend Michael, screaming for help, still reverberated within his mind.

Kayonga watched as Amaia led the way around the crater where a flash of yellow commanded their attention. As they drew closer, Kayonga's eyes widened at the sight of the grouping of several bright yellow, broad-leafed plants that grew out of dirt that consisted mainly of graphite. They extended much of the way around the nearer side of the crater.

Amaia went to one knee and reached out a gloved hand to run her fingers along the plants' fronds. "Look how bright these yellows are," Amaia said. "It's from the sulfur inside them." Kayonga knew that sulfur served the same function as oxygen in Earthly plants. Any animals that might exist on Lucy were expected, in turn, to use the sulfur from such plants as their equivalent of water.

As he watched Amaia examine the plants, one side of Kayonga's mouth turned upward in a wry smile. *I'm just glad to see there's something she can approve of,* he thought.

Amaia said, "I'm going to pick a couple samples and collect a series of readings." That was important, Kayonga knew, because life on Lucy was so different from the norm that it was difficult for their standard sensors to detect it; they had to establish baseline readings for future exploration. Amaia continued: "I'd like to be able to find some different plants or even some animals."

Kayonga, for his part, walked over to the side of the diamond-lined crater, which stood before him in its full glory. He marveled at the smoothness of the various facets of the diamonds forming its sides. *But then, that makes sense,* he thought. *What the hell is going to erode diamond?*

Then he noticed a black smudge on the arm of his life-suit. And another. He realized: *It's raining. I should've anticipated that. It makes sense it would rain more often here than on Earth -- carbon compounds need less energy to evaporate than water does. And rain here sure isn't water -- it can be methane, crude oil, or even something like tar.*

As he returned to Amaia, she was looking toward the sky. "I think it'll be too dangerous to go down in that crater in this oily rain. Even with a safety line, trying to get traction against diamond will be almost impossible."

Kayonga took a deep breath. *Much as I hate to admit it,* he thought, *she's right.* "Then I should help you with sensor readings on these plants."

"I'd appreciate that," Amaia said as she looked up at him. *And maybe she isn't smiling,* he thought, *but at least I'm not getting the usual scowl.* He lifted his left arm and activated the sensor cluster there. After completing his readings, Kayonga looked all around, taking in more details of the landscape. "Amaia," he said as he pointed toward the rise about twenty meters distant. "Does that look like a cave entrance to you?"

Amaia rose from her examination of plant life. "I believe you're right." She turned her wrist sensor in that direction. "And it's hard to tell, but this might be a life reading just inside it."

"More plants?"

"More complex, I think. Seeing signs of respiration -- nervous system activity. Likely . . . some kind of animal!"

"Now *that* we have to check out," Kayonga said.

Amaia didn't indicate agreement, just headed in that direction. Kayonga held his tongue as they approached the cave cautiously, he on the left and Amaia on the right.

They peered inside. The cave's ceiling rose just over the height of their heads. It extended far enough back that its walls quickly fell into darkness. Kayonga saw Amaia taking another lifesign reading. "Anything?" he asked.

"Yes, but still indeterminate."

Kayonga looked at Amaia. "We *have* to go in."

The oily rain splattered all around, including into the entrance to the hole. Amaia said, "It *is* tempting." She pressed more controls on her wrist scanner. "I'm extrapolating some of the readings from the plants. If I make some assumptions about animal life -- yes!"

Kayonga leaned forward. "What is it?"

"Three lifesigns."

"How big are they?"

"Not so big. About a meter and a half long, I'd say. Of course, we don't know how big their teeth might be. If they have teeth. Or claws."

Kayonga said, "I'd like to turn my palm light on, if you don't think it'll disturb whatever, whoever's in there."

Amaia considered that for a moment, then said, "Let's try that. I'll keep one eye on the sensor. If the readings take a jump in any value, I'll let you know."

Kayonga pointed his left palm toward the cave's interior and pressed his thumb into it, his heart racing. He leaned forward for a closer look within the hole.

And saw three pairs of eyes staring back.

Kayonga's mouth went dry. Talk about wonder! The

beings revealed within this hole were about a meter and a half long, as Amaia had said, roughly cylindrical, with four legs along each side, standing about eight meters within the cave. His voice was a mere croak as he said, "*Now* we've found something." The three creatures within the hole looked as if they were made up of finely woven silicon threads. The brilliance from his palm light reflected off their bodies in endless patterns. As they stared back at the Humans looking in at them, they hopped all around, against one another and the sides of the cave at first, then settled down against the rear of the cave, about five meters back from the entrance.

Amaia said, "Look how they shine! They're luminous! In fact, that's what we'll call them. Lumies!"

Kayonga shrugged. *Maybe the term won't stick*, he thought.

Amaia went on: "Do we dare go in for a closer look?"

"Let's not get too far ahead of ourselves," Kayonga said. "What if these are babies?"

Amaia took a deep breath, then let out a long sigh. "Meaning the mother might be nearby. You're right, of course."

Kayonga pressed his lips together. *A sentiment I never thought I'd hear her express. Though I shouldn't tell her that.*

Amaia continued: "Let's do a sweep of the entire area, then."

As they made the sensor sweep, Kayonga found himself more frustrated than anything. "It seems like something -- or someone's -- out there, but it's faint."

"I'm getting it, too," Amaia said. "Wait -- it's coming closer."

Kayonga pointed away from the cave. "There it is. Looks like an adult version of these little ones."

This new creature was about the size of a young black bear, with eight legs and similar thick silicon threads making up its body. Its face resembled a mask or a shell, and looked as if it were frozen into an angry grimace. As it approached, Kayonga pulled his stunner, telling Amaia, "We've got to protect ourselves."

Amaia grasped his arm, but didn't make him pull down his weapon. "We don't want to kill it."

"I'm set on the lowest stun cycle."

"Either way, don't be so eager to shoot something. You're not back at Jupiter."

"I wouldn't -- " Kayonga began, but stopped. *This isn't the time to rehash that,* he thought. Instead, he suggested, "We should move away from the cave. It -- or maybe she -- can only be interested in the babies. If that's what they are."

"Let's do that," Amaia said, and began stepping away from the cave. Kayonga followed, keeping his eyes on the mother the entire time.

But she turned toward him and Amaia. Kayonga saw a long line of sharp claws all along all eight of her paws. *And each of those legs,* he thought, *look pretty strong, as much as I can tell from their unusual physiology.*

"Shit," Kayonga said. It was about twenty meters away from them.

"Shit indeed," Amaia said, and now she pulled her stunner. She cast a grim look toward Kayonga and said, "We may have to shoot after all."

Fifteen meters.

Kayonga aimed his weapon at the adult lumie. "I'll do it."

"No," Amaia said. "This one's my responsibility."

Ten meters.

Amaia fired.

The shock of the beam striking the lumie made it pause. When it started forward again, its advance was slower, but no less certain. Amaia raised the stun level, fired again. The lumie paused again, but only for an instant. "It doesn't like the stunner," she said, "but it's not stopping."

Kayonga said, "We can't count on outrunning it to the shuttle, not through the tar."

Seven meters.

Amaia said, "We've got to go back to the cave."

"What? We can't -- "

"We can and we will. It's the only safe place for us." Amaia rushed back toward the cave entrance. Kayonga followed, careful not to slip on the thin film of crude oil the rain was leaving on the ground.

Five meters.

Kayonga followed Amaia, ducking into the cave, the lumie babies scrambling away from them. He turned to see if the adult lumie was halting its advance.

The lumie took a couple more steps, then stopped. Its shield-like head tilted to one side, then the other. "I think we've confused it," Kayonga said.

Amaia said, "It may be trying to figure out how to get to in here without us hurting its children."

Kayonga glanced back at the babies. Before, they'd been full of activity, hopping around in sheer abandon. Now they huddled together, all their eyes focused on these two strange Humans.

The adult lumie took a tentative step forward. Kayonga fired a stunner blast at its feet. It halted. "Seems capable of learning, anyway. You know, this is when we could've used the third person back aboard the shuttle."

Amaia said, "Yeah, well . . . I suppose we may have to look at that from now on."

Don't press it, Kayonga told himself, and kept quiet.

Amaia went on: "So what do we do now? I really don't

want to have to kill that thing. Especially if it just wants to protect its babies."

"Maybe we should just throw them out there. It gets what it wants, it leaves."

Amaia turned toward the babies. "Could be worth a shot." She reached for one of the small creatures. "C'mere, you." The lumie cowered against the cave wall. "Let's go see your mama out there." She grabbed the lumie and lifted it, as all eight of its legs paddled back and forth, as if it were swimming. "Damn thing's heavier than I anticipated in this grav," Amaia said as she moved toward the cave entrance. "Grab yourself one," she told Kayonga. "We'll send two at once."

As Kayonga stepped toward the back of the cave, a soft spot in the ground gave way and almost made him fall.

Balance, always balance. He grabbed up one of the lumie babies and went toward the front of the cave.

When its two babies came into sight, the adult lumie began to sway back and forth from one set of legs to the other. "We've got its attention," Amaia said. "Ready?"

Kayonga kept his eyes on the adult lumie as he held its offspring tight. "Ready."

"Push 'em out!"

Kayonga eased his lumie baby onto the concrete-like ground. Amaia did the same.

And each one ran right back into the cave.

The adult lumie took two steps forward, halted, then continued swaying back and forth.

Kayonga said, "So we're trapped in here, so are the babies, and their parent sure isn't going anywhere. Which means we not only have to get ourselves out of the cave safely, we have to get the babies out and keep them out. All without killing the mother."

Amaia's stare looked as if it would bore right through him.

"That's a lot to accomplish without anyone getting hurt. Assuaging your guilt, perhaps?"

Kayonga felt his face flush, but kept his voice calm. "No. That's not it."

"Why should I believe you?"

Kayonga forced himself to stand calmly, keep his fists from clenching. "Because nothing will ever lessen that guilt."

Amaia's voice sounded more sympathetic than he'd expected. "Oddly enough, I believe you."

"Well . . . I can only thank you for that."

"But I think of your actions then as a grand gesture. When you made it, the Jupiter whales lived, but two Humans died. I believe it's inherently dangerous . . . "

Kayonga said, "You sound as if . . . "

"Yes, I made a grand gesture of my own once."

"Care to tell me what it was?"

Amaia took so long to answer that Kayonga thought she'd decided not to speak. Finally, she said, "Have you ever heard of the old 'moral dilemma' test, where a person is placed on a chair with a noose around their neck? And a loved one is given a terrible choice to make?"

"No. I haven't."

"This happened just after the Great Human War." That was a conflict that had happened 48 years earlier, pitting Human against Human. Amaia continued: "I was the little girl standing on the chair, in front of a crowd of hostages. I was seven years old. The Star Rebellion loyalists told my mother if she didn't pull the chair out from under me, they would shoot one of the hostages. And if she didn't pull the chair, they would." Amaia's voice trailed away.

"So . . . what happened?"

"I was looking at my mother's back. I saw how she was standing. I could tell -- I could *tell* -- she was about to attack the guard. So I . . . I wanted my mother to live. I jumped off the chair."

Kayonga didn't dare make a sound.

"I was just starting to swing at the end of the rope. My mother didn't see me -- and the guard shot her."

"How did you -- "

"Some of the other prisoners grabbed me, held me up to keep the noose slack. We were rescued right after that. But it was too late for my mother."

Kayonga felt a lump growing in his throat. "I'm sorry you had to go through that."

"I appreciate that. But you see why I don't think the grand gesture works."

"I'll be very happy if we just muddle along." Kayonga indicated the three lumie babies at the rear of the cave. "Should we try again?"

"Can't hurt. Besides, making a single attempt and giving up isn't very scientific, is it?"

"Here we go, then." Kayonga stepped back toward the rear of the cave --

-- As part of the cave floor collapsed beneath him and his right leg fell through the hole. "Oh, shit!" He spread his arms wide and caught himself as the hole widened and his left leg also dangled in mid-air.

Amaia was by Kayonga's side immediately, grabbing him beneath his arms and helping pull him from the hole. He scooted on his backside away from the hole before he stood up. He leaned forward, turned on his palm light, and peered downward. "Looks like some sort of cavity opened up."

As Amaia came up beside him to have a look, Kayonga grasped her arm. "Careful. This thing's getting wider."

Amaia took a step back and began taking sensor readings. "We're a bit heavier than the babies are. Perhaps their parent never actually came in here. Looks like quite a cavern beneath us. We wouldn't survive the fall." She indicated the lumie babies. "I'd bet they wouldn't either."

"So the list gets longer. We need to get the babies out of here and keep them from running back in. We have to get ourselves out without the mother attacking us. And without us having to kill the mother."

"And before the rest of the cave floor collapses."

"Much as I hate to say it," Kayonga told Amaia, "it may be time for a grand gesture."

Amaia emitted a deep sigh. "Let's hear it."

"We grab the babies, throw them right toward the mother. One of us ups their stunner to blaster status."

"To protect us against the lumie mother?"

"No, to seal the entrance to this cave after we leave it."

"So where do we go?"

"Someplace very shiny."

Amaia said, "You don't mean -- "

"Yes, I do. Let's get ready."

Kayonga couldn't help but keep glancing at the lumie mother as he and Amaia made their preparations. He stepped carefully around the hole in the cave floor to fill his arms with all three of the lumie babies. Amaia set her weapon to blaster status.

Finally they stood together at the cave entrance. "At least the rain's stopped," Kayonga said as he tried to hold onto three squirming lumie babies. "Ready?"

"As I'll ever be," Amaia replied.

"Then let's go."

Kayonga, bracing himself against the one-third stronger grav, took three long strides toward the lumie mother. In the same instant, Amaia turned her weapon toward the cave entrance and fired. Its beam blasted the cave's ceiling, sending debris everywhere and blocking its entrance.

Kayonga dumped the lumie babies onto the ground about five meters in front of their mother.

Then he and Amaia ran as fast as they could toward the diamond crater, and slid into the bowl.

Kayonga was first over the side. The nanotech in his life-suit hardened against the repeated impacts of his body against the many sharp facets of the diamond walls, but he still took a pounding.

The stronger grav made his descent more rapid than it would have been on Earth. The remnants of the oily rainfall lining the crater's walls sped him along even faster.

Finally, he reached bottom, his body rocking back and forth a couple of times before settling down in a puddle of oil at the bottom of the crater.

Kayonga heard, as if from a distant room, Amaia shouting his name. He groaned as he raised himself up on his elbows and tried to focus his attention. The impression that the crater was swirling around him made him think better of that idea.

Amaia's shouts became more insistent. "Kayonga! How are you?"

He opened his eyes and saw her leaning over him. "All right, I guess. How are you?"

"OK. It was a heck of a ride." She pointed upward, toward the rim of the crater. "And our friend followed us that far."

Kayonga made another attempt to raise himself up, and this one worked. The many facets of the diamonds lining the crater reflected a myriad of flashing points, and stood out in much more detailed relief from this viewpoint. He looked upward, across the twenty meters of rain-slick diamond between him and the top of the crater. The lumie mother looked as if she was teetering on its edge.

Amaia said, "If she comes down here, it's all over. We'll have to shoot to kill."

"We have to keep her from wanting to come down her in the first place," Kayonga said as he pulled his stunner. He dialed it down to the least harmful setting and the widest beam. *This has to work*, he thought. *I don't have any more ideas.*

Kayonga braced himself as best he could against the slippery diamond floor of the crater. He aimed his stunner, not at the enraged mother, but in the opposite direction, toward the diamond-layered crater wall. He told Amaia, "Close your eyes!"

He squeezed his eyelids tight and fired.

A silent explosion of light, visible even through Kayonga's eyelids, cast itself across the crater and onto the landscape around the mother. Any stun effect on her, he hoped, was diffused.

Kayonga opened his eyes.

"That was genius, Kayonga," Amaia told him. The mother was hanging back from the crater rim, shaking her head and blinking her eyes. "I hope you didn't blind her."

"Better than killing her. And, look!"

The lumie mother gave Kayonga and Amaia what appeared to be, even across the species divide, a disgusted glance. *She can see just fine*, Kayonga thought. She scooted away from the crater, her brood close behind.

Amaia said, "I guess the grand gesture works sometimes, after all."

Kayonga took a moment to consider what to say. Then: "Everything is circumstance. The last 'grand gesture' I tried, I couldn't save everyone. This time, we could. But I had an advantage. You were here to help."

Amaia said, "I was unfair to you. And I know why. I was afraid. Not so much for myself, but that I'd have to let those babies die or kill the mother or -- *something*. And then have to live with that fact, every day of the rest of my life. So I understand what you went through back at Jupiter -- what you're still going through."

"I . . . appreciate that."

"We'd better get back to the shuttle."

Kayonga asked, "Are we headed back up to the ship?"

"*Hell*, no. A chance to rest, to calibrate our sensors to detect the more intelligent and dangerous lifeforms here, and then it's right back out. Oh, and one more thing."

Kayonga tilted his head. "What's that?"

Amaia slapped him on the shoulder. "I'll let Captain Marianthal know the tryouts are over. I've got my new partner."

Kayonga and Amaia began the delicate climb up the countless diamond facets lining the wall of the crater. By the time they reached the top, the lumies were gone.

On the way across the tarry portion of the landscape near the shuttle's landing site, Kayonga began his negotiation with the planet's surface again.

This time, though, the screams reverberating in Kayonga's mind dimmed just enough to allow a smile to reveal itself behind his faceplate.

How to maintain the welcome relief underlying that emotion? Concentrate on advancing across this sticky landscape beneath these shrouded skies. Lift one foot *this* much, lean forward *that* much, and balance, always balance.

Short on Thought, Quick on the Trigger

Here's a quick little adventure involving Carrie Molina that still manages to fill in a bit of her backstory. Oddly enough, it's the only one of the three stories in this collection in which we get to see her special abilities in action.

———

Carrie Molina grabbed Bennie Delgado's arm and all but dragged him down the smoke-filled corridor of the science facility on the planet Anaktuvuk. "The bio-alert is fake," she told him as he stumbled along beside her. "So's the smoke."

Bennie started to ask, "Who set it -- "

"*I* did," Carrie said, as she kept a close eye on doorways and intersecting corridors. "The Sobrenians' protocols in an emergency send most of them to their command center."

"Great job! Gimme a disruptor."

"Sorry, only a stunner. Reach into my backpack."

Carrie felt his hands rummaging through the pack. "Hold still," he said.

"Grab while we run. We've got to get to the water." *We're already taking too long*, Carrie thought. *My lungs have shrunk again, my heart rate's slowing down. Although the sight of even one Sobrenian might bring it right back up again.* The Sobrenians were a warlike species that considered weapons technology its greatest art form.

"Got it!" Bennie said. They started down a side corridor that was free of smoke. Once again the air had the slightly sweet smell of Sobrenian atmosphere. Bennie continued: "You know, I can't help but notice how great you look in that skinsuit -- "

"Don't bother noticing. Just because we used to have sex doesn't give you any privileges."

"Hey, I just -- "

"I'm getting your ass out of here and that's all."

"Look out!" Bennie said as he fired across Carrie's shoulder at a Sobrenian who was rushing away from them. The Sobrenian's body fell with a deep thud. It had a torso three times the thickness of a Human's, a blunt snout, and rough skin.

Carrie fought to keep her anger down. "That was one of the scientists," she told him. "You didn't have to shoot him."

"He'll wake up soon enough."

Same old Bennie, she thought. *Short on thought, quick on the trigger.*

The Earth Unity had sent Carrie to Anaktuvuk to rescue Bennie from this abandoned Human facility. Before his capture, Bennie had sent word that the Sobrenians were committing scientific research that involved killing hundreds of members of a sentient aquatic species, the Enahle, native to Anaktuvuk's oceans.

Carrie's job was to extract Bennie from that facility before the Sobrenians could use him to spark a diplomatic incident.

Because Humans had built the Anaktuvuk facility, Carrie

was able to figure out how to trigger the fake bio-alert and fill many of the facility's corridors with smoke. That, in turn, let her stun the only guard standing outside the makeshift cell where the Sobrenians were holding Bennie, and free him.

Figuring out Bennie himself was something Carrie had given up on long ago.

Another intersection of corridors, and Carrie pointed to the right. "This way."

Bennie said, "The other way takes us outside quicker."

Carrie pushed him to the right. "You forget who you're dealing with. The ocean's this way."

Three Sobrenians came around a corner to their left. They quickly pulled weapons and began firing at Carrie and Bennie.

Bennie went to one knee and returned fire, Carrie standing over him doing the same. Two of the Sobrenians fell immediately. The third ran back around the corner.

The corridor ended at a doorway leading onto a balcony. As Carrie and Bennie stepped outside, Anaktuvuk's only moon, Kokogiaq, shone bright in the night sky. The balcony stood at the top of a sheer cliff overlooking the wave-rippled sea thirty meters below.

Bennie hugged himself and stamped his feet. The entire planet was too cold for comfort for Humans, as it was entering a period of runaway glaciation. "You could'a brought a coat for me, you know," he told Carrie.

"Never mind that," she said as she slipped her backpack off her shoulders just long enough to pull out a breathing mask. "Put this on."

He did, then stuck his stunner into his belt. "Oh, I got it. Your shuttle's down there."

"Sort of. Actually, it's over the horizon."

"Wait a minute -- what?"

Several heavily-armed Sobrenians were running down the corridor toward them.

Carrie told Bennie, "Now turn around."

Bennie said, "What the hell are you -- " Carrie, her patience exhausted, grabbed Bennie by the shoulders and turned him away from her. She pressed her body against his back.

"Hey," Bennie said, "this would be more fun if we faced each other."

"Bennie, just shut up," Carrie said as her skinsuit extruded itself over Bennie's body as well as her own.

"Wait a minute, you can't be -- "

"I can be, and I am," Carrie said as she lifted one leg over the edge of the balcony, Bennie's body going along with her.

"Don't tell me we're going to -- "

"Don't tell me what I can't do," Carrie said as she swung her other leg over the balcony's edge.

"But I can't swim!"

Taking as deep a breath as she could and holding Bennie tight, she propelled the both of them off the balcony.

Bennie screamed all the way down.

Their combined skinsuit protected Carrie and Bennie from most of the impact with the water. They pierced a large grouping of Enahle, and a dozen or more of them scattered in all directions. They were sleek creatures longer and slimmer than a dolphin, with bright alert eyes. *I swear I can sense the intelligence behind those eyes,* Carrie thought. *The idea that anyone would kill them, for any reason, is beyond my way of thinking.*

Carrie felt Bennie tense up as she held him tight. *Where are those smart-ass remarks now?* she thought.

Even the skinsuit would slow her down now; with a quick squeeze of her left hand into a fist, it flowed away from her body while maintaining a breathing unit over her face and continuing to protect Bennie.

With Carrie's body exposed directly to the water, her heart pumped blood more rapidly to keep her warm. Micro-dermal ridges along her skin allowed her to glide through the water with less resistance. Her lungs expanded to half-again their usual size, though the breather made that of less importance than usual. *I fully expect Bennie to make a comment about my breasts growing bigger, though,* she thought.

Carrie pumped her legs furiously, sending her and Bennie deeper and deeper into Anaktuvuk's waters. Curiously, many of the Enahle followed.

From above came flashes of Sobrenian gunfire -- energy bolts, mostly ineffective once they struck water. *Guess they didn't expect a bio-engineered Human to make this rescue,* she thought.

Even her own abilities wouldn't be enough to save them, though. Another squeeze, this time with her right fist, and the propulsion unit in her backpack activated, sending her and Bennie swiftly through the sea. They soon left the group of Enahle behind.

Bennie spoke through the breather's comlink: "Couldn't they have sent a bunch of Unity Marines to get me out?"

"You know how that goes, Bennie. Diplomacy."

"I guess I should just be glad they sent you, huh, Carriden? I guess we understand each other."

If you understood me that well, Carrie thought, *you'd remember how much I hate being called by my full name.* She and Bennie had grown up in the same neighborhood in Madrid. At eight years old, he was the one who dared her to climb higher and higher on a tree in her own backyard, despite her nearly over-whelming fear. At eleven, he was the one who snuck her two full glasses of wine during a party at his parents' house. The

resulting headache the next morning sent her back to the occa-
sional parent-approved sips.

At sixteen, Bennie admitted he'd been looking at Carrie
with different eyes for some time and wanted to see if touching
her matched his new perceptions.

She declined the offer.

For one day.

After a few months, college beckoned Carrie, then the
stars. Bennie moved to the Earth-orbital Shosha Habitat.

Now, seventeen years later, they arrived at Carrie's
submersible shuttle. Carrie let Bennie go. As they waited for
the submersible's lock to cycle, several of the Enahle caught up
with them. They swam all around the two of them, but one
drew close to Bennie, took up stationkeeping right next to him,
and stared intently at him. Carrie could tell this encounter
frightened Bennie; he windmilled his arms and legs to try to
ease away from the Enahle, but the Enahle, with a couple
casual flips of its fins, stayed right with him.

"I think it likes you," Carrie said.

"Well, I don't like it! We gotta get inside!"

The submersible's outer lock opened. Carrie reached for
Bennie to guide him inside. With another flip of its fins, the
Enahle lunged forward and its snout punched Bennie in
the gut.

Bennie's arms and legs flailed around even more. "Get me
the hell inside!" he shouted.

Carrie came up behind Bennie and shoved him into the
lock. She took a last glance back at the Enahle that had
assaulted Bennie. A dozen or more others lined themselves up
behind it. *They know something*, Carrie thought. *And I have a pretty
good idea what it is.*

The water level lowered all too slowly in the submersible's
lock. A combination of hot blasts of air and a burst of sonics

dried them within moments. Bennie's fear vanished from his features as he leered at Carrie's nude body. A squeeze of her left hand, and her skinsuit established itself again. Bennie shook his head. "So disappointing," he said.

"You had your chance years ago," Carrie said. "You went in a different direction." She'd kept track of Bennie after he went to live on Shosha Habitat. Its inhabitants lived under a market economy, instead of a post-scarcity replicator economy like most Human societies. By all accounts, he'd thrived there. But she'd heard too many times of shady deals, stiffed clients, and sudden disappearances when bills came due.

As Carrie and Bennie stepped through the inner lock and into the submersible's main cabin, Bennie asked, "What shuttle is this?"

"*Devries*. Out of *Kojima*. It's hiding behind Anaktuvuk's moon."

"A military ship? Why didn't they just stage a full-fledged raid?"

"The last thing the Unity wants is to get into a shooting match over you."

Bennie's shoulders slumped and he let his arms fall to his sides. He looked toward the floor. "I guess I should be glad anyone came to get me at all." He looked up at Carrie. "Thanks for that. I don't know what the Sobrenians would've done to me."

"Their military wanted to *kill* you. Didn't you know that?"

"I was worried about that, but -- "

"*But* -- their scientists wanted to bury the whole thing. They were afraid your accusations would cause a scandal, which would lead to budget cuts. They wanted you gone and forgotten."

Bennie shrugged. "Guess I should be glad the scientists won out."

Carrie couldn't make herself look at Bennie for a moment. Finally she took a deep breath and said, "I know what you did. What the Sobrenians found you doing."

Bennie's gaze narrowed, and his voice lost its friendly lilt. "What does that mean, Carrie?"

"Where's *your* shuttle, Bennie?"

"Had to scuttle it. The Sobrenians were bearing down on me."

"What about those Enahle? They didn't seem to like you very much."

Bennie spread his hands wide. "How should I know? They're just animals."

"They're considered sentient, about like dolphins on Earth, or Jupiter whales."

"I don't like what you seem to be saying -- "

"I know what you did, Bennie. People on Shosha Habitat think the ground-up bones of the Enahle are an aphrodisiac. You were killing them and stripping them of their flesh, leaving just the bones."

"You can't know that!"

"I notice you didn't deny it. I went to your shuttle first, Bennie. You didn't scuttle it. It's sitting on that island where you created the rendering facility. That's why the Enahle chased us. That's why the one attacked you. That's where the Sobrenians found you."

"As if the Sobrenians care about the Enahle," Bennie said.

"They've certainly committed their share of atrocities. But even they don't want to be accused of one they didn't do."

"The Unity -- "

"The Unity wanted you gone, too. They wanted the Sobrenians to owe Humanity a favor. "

Bennie's body tensed up. "And since the Sobrenians were inhabiting a former Human facility -- "

"I knew how to get in there and get you out. The Sobre-nians aren't going to admit their own incompetence. They'll never speak of you again."

"Carrie, I can't believe this. We meant something to each other once."

Memories lanced through Carrie's consciousness: *Bennie daring her to climb higher and higher. That first hangover. That first night in bed. Damn, he was good.*

"I'm sorry," was all she could manage to say.

Bennie slowly pulled out his stunner. "I guess I'm sorry, too." He squeezed the trigger.

The stunner didn't fire.

"I'm disappointed, Bennie," Carrie said. "Not that you tried to shoot me. That you thought I was stupid enough not to set that stunner to deactivate the moment we came into the shuttle."

Bennie tried to rush Carrie, but she'd anticipated that and when she squeezed her own stunner's trigger, it fired. Bennie slumped to the floor.

Carrie sighed. *Should'a made him sit down first. Now I gotta drag him into the jump seat and strap him in.*

Typical. Now I'm the one short on thought, quick on the trigger. Bennie always was a bad influence.

Sungazers

Here's yet another story featuring Carrie Molina, and this time she faces a moral dilemma worthy of Kayonga Tedesco.

I wonder whether I've arrived just in time to see the start of an interplanetary war, Carrie Molina thought as eight Cetronen starcraft descended through the clear southern skies of the Human-colonized planet Costaguana. The mottled blue-and-black craft stood over a hundred meters tall, their gravitic drives bringing them down smoothly, despite a sharp crosswind, toward the dusty plain they'd chosen as their landing site.

A force of nearly a hundred Earth Unity Marines awaited the Cetronen's arrival, having arrived in two large personnel shuttles from the Unity starcraft *Admiral Susan Kojima*, in orbit around Costaguana. The Marines stood a couple of rows deep in a quarter-circle around the landing site, weapons at the ready but carefully not pointed at the descending ships.

About five kilometers behind them to the north, past a

thick grove of braidwood trees, was the Human settlement of Green Town, home to several hundred people. Several families also occupied farms between the landing site and the town.

The scary part, Carrie thought, *is that Colonel Eisler seems to be deferring to me. But I'm a "fixer," not a diplomat. I'm used to working behind the scenes, or even in secret. I'm expected to break the rules if needed, not necessarily to uphold them.*

We were told this was supposed to be just one Cetronen ship making a friendly visit, not a small fleet of them. And our sensors haven't been able to get any readings on what -- or who -- might be inside those ships.

The Marines' commander, Colonel Norman Eisler, a dour presence with melancholy features, told Carrie, "My instructions from the Unity were to let the Cetronen set down peacefully, then react as needed."

"I hope you don't have to react at all," Carrie said.

One by one, the Cetronen craft touched down on tiny insectile legs and settled into place, raising thick dust clouds that largely obscured them. The ships' final stances, precarious as they appeared, gave Carrie no sense that the giant craft were in any danger of teetering over.

Carrie heard the scrape of metal against metal, of the rustling of body armor against clothing. Marines tensing, anticipating. "Tighten it up," Col. Eisler said. "Keep it still."

The scraping and rustling sounds cut off.

No sound, no movement from the Cetronen craft.

Carrie turned to Col. Eisler. "What do we do now?"

"One of the toughest things a soldier or diplomat can do."

"Ah! Wait?"

Col. Eisler's face, framed by his helmet, made a humorless smile. "You're catching on."

Within a minute, though, the underside of the nearest Cetronen craft opened up and a wide ramp extended down to the Costaguanan surface. Several Cetronen pairs came down that ramp, each of the majors carrying their minors. Cetronen were paired symbionts; the two-and-a-half meter tall majors were designed for strength and endurance, with the smaller minors perched on the majors' bellies being more intelligent. They all took position to either side of the ramp.

The other Cetronen ships followed suit, with ramps extending and Cetronen pairs lining up next to them.

"What the hell is this?" Carrie asked. "Some sort of honor guard?"

The answer came moments later as other beings appeared at the tops of the ramps. They were about the same height as the Cetronen majors. Skin the color of earth. Thin legs. Arms thin as well, with four segments that reached down to the beings' knees. Dark green wings were folded against their backs.

Carrie knew she had to be staring wide-eyed and slack-jawed, but didn't care; she was amazed by the sight before her.

These beings had thin necks that supported narrow heads. Some had tufts of hair right above their recessed ears, others were bald. They filed out of the Cetronen craft and about half of them gathered side-by-side in several rows, like troops on review, facing the Cetronen craft. The others formed a circle around them, facing outwards. Those in the middle raised their arms, revealing more of the broad dark green wings that stretched from their fingertips to their calves. Those wings were thinly etched with veins of a lighter green. The beings presented their wings to the late afternoon sun. The beings forming the circle stood passively facing outward, wings still folded.

Carrie and Col. Eisler shared a glance. The Marine colonel said, "It looks like they've circled the wagons."

Carrie's eyebrows narrowed. "Huh?"

"They've formed a defensive perimeter."

"Doesn't look like it would be much of a defense against your Marines."

Col. Eisler lowered his helmet's lenses and touched a control. "You may be right. We don't know how advanced these folks with the wings are. This may be something pre-tech, even an instinct."

"The ones inside their perimeter look like they're sunning themselves. Maybe even soaking up energy?"

"Could be. Oh, look." The colonel pointed to a Cetronen pair who was breaking ranks from his post next to the closest ship's ramp and was approaching the Humans. "An emissary, maybe?"

"Dammit," Carrie said. "I guess I'd better be the one to approach him."

"I'm sure the Unity would prefer that."

As Carrie walked to intercept the Cetronen, she thought, *The Unity would prefer a lot of shit that ain't gonna happen.*

The Earth Unity had been considerably weakened by the recent Jenregar incursion on Earth. The conflict hadn't lasted long, but it had been hard-fought, killing several million people and ravaging many of Earth's cities and much of its infrastructure.

One of those millions had been Carrie's father, who'd died a torturous death at the Jenregar's hands. Her only consolation was that neither her mother nor sister, who had died years earlier, had been there to witness it.

The Unity's focus is close to home right now, Carrie thought. *The colonel and I can do all the bitching and hand-waving we want, and nothing's going to happen.*

Human and Cetronen stopped about two meters from one another. The Cetronen major carried the minor on a hump on his belly. The major had wide pointed ears, a thin mouth, and no nose. His eyes were deep-set beneath a jutting brow. A thick tail helped balance the being.

The minor was a smaller, thinner version of the major, and did the talking: "I am Golareg. I am to be the liaison between my people and the Humans here on the world you call Costaguana."

"I am Carrie Molina. I . . . represent the Earth Unity here." *I'm not about to explain what a "fixer" is,* she thought.

"You are not an ambassador?"

"Only a few hundred Humans live here. The population's purposely been kept small. And this world isn't a cultural or trade hub. The Unity hasn't seen the need to establish an ambassador."

The minor indicated the force of Marines all around. "The Unity seems quick enough to make a military response."

"The Unity was told just one Cetronen ship would be visiting."

The minor said, "This is a situation in which we may want to speak more privately. It involves . . . an unfortunate time in the history of my species."

Col. Eisler said, "We can go over to *Devries.*" That shuttle and another one, the *Minsky,* were the personnel shuttles that had brought the Marines down from the orbiting *Kojima.*

As Carrie, Golareg, and the colonel started toward the shuttle, Carrie nodded toward the gathering of winged beings outside the Cetronen ships. "We also weren't told there would be other visitors."

The minor's body shook in a way that Carrie knew indicated laughter. "These are not visitors," he said. "These are the original natives of Costaguana, who have come to take back their planet from Humanity."

Within moments, Carrie, Golareg, and Col. Eisler shut themselves away within the small galley of the shuttle *Devries*. The Golareg major didn't sit, so Carrie and Col. Eisler remained standing, as well. The Golareg minor, of course, remained perched on the major's stomach hump.

"So tell us," Carrie said, "how the hell these beings could originally be from Costaguana."

The Golareg minor said, "In a strict sense, they are not. They do, however, represent our successful attempt to, you might say, reverse-engineer them."

Col. Eisler took a deep breath and Carrie could tell he was holding his anger back. "And what the hell does *that* mean?"

"Have your researchers not found the fossil evidence of these beings here?"

"Most of the Humans settling here are trained in the arts," Carrie said. "They're musicians and writers and artists. They've never started a serious effort to look at the fossil record. We just knew there wasn't any intelligent life here *now*."

Col. Eisler said, "I think we're skirting past an important point. What did you mean by an 'unfortunate' time in Cetronen history?"

Golareg's minor folded his hands on his lap. His eyes wouldn't meet those of the two Humans. "We . . . committed genocide. Here on this planet."

Carrie asked, "You mean, against the original versions of these beings you've brought back?"

"The original native Costaguanans, yes. This is our enduring shame. Something we have kept from the other Galactic species we've made contact with."

"Why did it happen?"

Golareg's minor sat silently for a moment, and Carrie wondered if he would even respond. Finally he said, "It was almost two hundred years ago. We had just developed stardrive and a great many of us thought we were destined to colonize this part of the galaxy. When we came here, we found an indigenous species that couldn't fight back."

Col. Eisler made a sweeping gesture. "So you just killed them?"

"It was not a consensus within our species. In fact, some Cetronen craft from a rival faction arrived to try to stop the genocide. A lot of that conflict played out in orbit. However, the Cetronen who wanted to kill all the native Costaguanans prevailed."

Carrie asked, "So how did you recreate them?"

"Our scientists of the time took many tissue samples, and even entire bodies, back to our homeworld to study. Please, all we Cetronen ask is that you do not judge our entire species by the actions of our ancestors from two centuries ago."

Carrie looked at Col. Eisler. "I suppose we don't have a lot of leeway to talk, there. Two centuries ago for Humanity? World War Two. Naked bodies piled up at Buchenwald. Hell, not even fifty years ago. The Great Human War. Charred bones piled up at Luwero."

Golareg's minor said, "Thankfully, attitudes among my people shifted. This is a time we now see as shameful. We know that in returning these beings to their homeworld, we cannot erase that shame. But we hope to mitigate it."

Col. Eisler said, "But now we have Human settlements here. And these native Costaguanans are supposed to make everyone leave? This could be considered an invasion against a Human colony."

"You cannot invade your own homeworld," Golareg's minor said.

Carrie asked, "What's proper when two groups of people claim the same homeland? Can we talk to these native Costaguanans?"

"They think of themselves as 'Sungazers.' And yes, several of them have been given datalinks programmed to interpret Cetronen and Human speech. I can, in turn, provide the programming for their speech to you."

Col. Eisler said, "I'll get my people on that quick as I can."

"Tell me about these people," Carrie said. "Are they actually soaking up sunlight for energy with those wings?"

"They are," Golareg's minor said.

"But the time that would take each day -- "

"No more than many predators take in the hunt, and in resting afterwards."

Col. Eisler said, "Speaking of predators, I suppose the ones taking in sunlight would be easy prey if it weren't for the ones guarding them."

"That is exactly right. After several hours, the two groups switch, with those previously absorbing energy becoming the guards."

Carrie said, "You stated pretty bluntly that they're here to take this planet back from Humanity. Do you think they have any wiggle room on that at all?"

"Failure to translate."

"Sorry. Idiom. Would they be willing to negotiate?"

"They have never met a Human before. They will know you only as trespassers."

Col. Eisler said, "They could also come to know us as people determined to protect our homes. Humans have settled a very small portion of this planet, Ambassador. There's room for everyone."

The Golareg minor said, "They consider Humanity's presence on their world as you would a cancer within your own body. Would you leave that cancer alone? The Sungazers are here to stay, Colonel. Unless the Unity is willing to commit a second genocide against them. Not to mention risking conflict between the Unity and the Cetronen. Would that be wise, particularly as the Unity is recovering from the Jenregar incursion?"

"With all respect," Carrie said, "let's not argue the point in here. Let's take it out to the Sungazers."

———

Carrie rubbed behind her left ear, where Human technicians had just implanted an update to her datalink's translation protocols. Those techs were confident that Carrie and Col. Eisler, and any other Human provided with that update, would be able to communicate with the Sungazers as they would any other Galactic species.

Carrie couldn't honestly say she itched where the techs had made the injection. But every time she thought of what was at stake, she ended up scratching behind that ear.

"I'll stay behind for now," Col. Eisler told Carrie. "I'd say it's best to take a peaceful stance with this first contact."

"You're probably right," Carrie said. She and Golareg proceeded toward the dozens of Sungazers just outside the nearest Cetronen ship. Their inner rows tilted their wings toward the setting sun.

Golareg's minor told Carrie, "When we re-created the Sungazers, we raised them on our homeworld for several generations. Cetronen cared for the first generation, and we taught that Sungazer generation to care for the next."

"It sounds as if you took a cautious approach."

"We had never undertaken such a project. To teach another species how to care for itself, how to raise families, maintain social groups -- it's quite difficult. Especially when that species is so alien to us. The way they feed, and of course the fact that they are . . . well . . . . "

Carrie suggested, "Singletons?" She knew that some Cetronen held prejudices against other Galactic species who were not paired symbionts. In other words, all other known Galactic species.

Golareg's minor said, "If the term does not offend."

As much as Carrie could tell from a being with a largely immobile face, no nose, and cavernous eyes, Golareg was genuinely unwilling to hurt anyone's feelings. She said, "I understand the objective meaning of the term, Ambassador. There are other Humans who would not be so charitable."

They paused just outside the outer circle of Sungazers. Golareg's minor said, "We must be careful to approach to one side of those who are facing the sun. Come from behind them, and they may fear a sneak attack, despite the circle of guards. In front of them, and we would block the sunlight, which would be impolite."

Carrie looked toward the Sungazers. The individuals in the outer ring were tilting their heads and squinting in their lidless way to get a better look at her and Golareg. Those in the inner rows still faced the sun.

This could be the most important moment in the Human relationship with the Sungazers, Carrie thought. *If we can't talk with them, we'll only be able to communicate through overt actions, and those are prone to misunderstandings that can lead to violence.*

Carrie squeezed her hands together. This was *not* the time for nervousness or fear.

The sun was slipping below the horizon. The individuals within the inner rows of Sungazers lowered their wings slowly. *Almost,* Carrie thought, *reverently.*

"Let me lead the way," the Golareg minor said. "I will attempt the first communication. As you listen in, you'll learn whether these first attempts at an accurate translation have been successful. Keep in mind, their vocalizations are guttural, yet nuanced in tone, and generated as much by stomach muscles as by vocal cords. They also emit low-level electric fields that add to the meaning of words."

Carrie was trying to focus on what Golareg was saying, but felt slightly dizzy and she was breathing in quick, nervous inhalations. *Damn*, she thought, *I'm about to hyperventilate if I'm not careful.* She forced herself to breathe more slowly and told Golareg, "Try to tell them our intentions are peaceful."

The Golareg major halted and the minor looked to the Sungazers. They all turned to face him. Carrie felt dwarfed by both Golareg and the Sungazers. *When you're the shortest being in the bunch*, she thought, *it's easy to feel a little insecure.*

The Golareg minor spread his arms wide. "I greet the Sungazers as they revel in the rediscovery of their homeworld."

The slender Sungazers stood with their long, four-segmented arms hanging at their sides. Their three-fingered hands were level with their knees. Carrie saw no change of expression in any of those dozens of lidless eyes or their broad, square-jawed mouths.

Carrie heard the soft spongegrass rustling as one of the Sungazers who had been gathering sunlight in the inner rows stepped forward. He stopped before Golareg and stared. With the sun farther beneath the horizon, it was difficult for Carrie to make out the male's features, and she fought to resist the temptation of speaking up herself, of breaking the tension this staring contest evoked within her by *doing* something.

Carrie feared it was at least a 50-50 chance that she'd do something wrong. It was Golareg who had the experience here, and she had to defer to his judgment for now.

The Sungazer spoke.

His voice was a rumble that came up from within his body, generated by the stomach muscles Golareg had just mentioned. Knowing the Sungazer was also generating a low-level electrical field, Carrie could have sworn her hair was trying to stand on end. A quick swipe across the top of her head told her that effect was psychosomatic at best.

And over her datalink . . . .

"*Skrrrk . . . skraaak . . . .* " Then silence.

Carrie said in a stage whisper to Golareg, "That's it?"

The Golareg major turned his body so the minor could face Carrie. "And they say Cetronen are an impatient species. It takes more than a single sentence to refine the programming."

Carrie frowned. "Sorry," he muttered. "What did he say?"

"He returned my greetings. But I am not here to translate for you." The Golareg major turned his back on Carrie. The minor asked the Sungazer, "May I ask your name?"

Again, all Carrie heard was "*Skrrrk . . . .* "

The major turned toward Carrie again. The minor said, "I suppose you didn't perceive that."

"No," Carrie said.

The Golareg minor folded his arms in an inadvertent imitation of his major's stance that Carrie would've found amusing any other time.

"Very well, then," the minor said. "This Sungazer's name is Arda. He is the leader of his tribe."

Carrie stared upward at the tall being who regarded her with mysterious, hooded eyes. "Pleased to meet you, Arda."

The Golareg minor said, "Arda cannot understand you, either, unfortunately. This may require some time." The major turned back toward the Sungazers and the minor went on with his conversation, which continued to sound to Carrie like a series of squawks and squeaks.

It was difficult to see Golareg's face -- either face -- in the remaining dim glow from the west. The larger moon, Wait, wouldn't rise for another few minutes, and the smaller one, Marlow, not for an hour after that.

I suppose, Carrie thought, *I can only hope Golareg's not telling Arda that Humans are the devils of the universe.*

Finally Golareg's minor said, "I have finished our initial conversation."

Carrie asked, "And?"

"I began with a personal plea. I spoke in my own species' interest, telling Arda of the Cetronen desire to maintain the relationship the Sungazers and Cetronen enjoyed on our homeworld. I also made an honest attempt, I assure you, to explain the Human desire to learn more about the Sungazer species."

"Ambassador, I need to communicate these things on my own. When can we expect a working translator?"

"These things take time. I suggest you continue to engage Arda in conversation. The translator tech learns by experience. The more real-time language protocols it's subjected to, the more efficient it becomes."

Carrie walked past Golareg and started toward the Sungazers. "Fine, let's talk! Arda!"

The tall tribal leader looked down with baleful eyes at Carrie, who held her arms out toward the Sungazer. "Arda, each of our species needs to learn more about the other. We may have to share this planet. Humanity came here thinking there had never been intelligent life on Costaguana. Sungazers were all but destroyed by the Cetronen, but now you've returned. Perhaps we can live side by side."

Arda didn't speak, only continued to regard Carrie with -- amusement? Contempt? Carrie had no way of knowing. *How powerful,* she wondered, *are those thin, four-segmented Sungazer arms, those three-fingered hands? How quick? If Arda wanted to grasp me by the neck and make a clean snap, could he do it?*

Carrie heard another low rumble and realized it was Arda speaking directly to her. At first squawking sounds dominated still, but then she started hearing phrases that made sense: "*Skrrrk* . . . pleasure. *Serrekkk* . . . secure our rightful . . . . *Yrrr nemmmm* . . . What *issss* . . . your name?"

Carrie favored Golareg with a broad smile. "You did it!"

The Golareg minor said, "You needn't sound so surprised. Would I be eager to portray my species as less than competent?"

Carrie turned back to Arda. "I'm Carrie Molina, a . . . representative of the Earth Unity."

Arda stared down intently at Carrie. "As Golareg told you, I am Arda, tribal chief."

"I'm eager to communicate more with you. Should I address you as tribal chief, or some other title?"

"That is not necessary. I am Arda. We demand that you admit this is the Sungazers' world, and that Humanity will not be allowed to continue living here."

Carrie stood with hands clenched. "That's an extreme position to take. Humanity has established itself on this planet for a number of years."

"Ambassador Golareg and the other Cetronen have educated us on Humanity's attitudes toward worlds it inhabits."

"Arda, with all respect, in my experience with other cultures I've learned it's best to learn about another people by interacting directly with them, and not taking the word, however well-intentioned -- " She nodded politely toward Golareg. " -- of others."

"My experience is that other cultures have nothing to teach Sungazers."

Even given that Arda was a member of a low-tech, nonspacefaring species, Carrie found that surprising. "Did your friends the Cetronen teach you nothing?"

"They taught us that Sungazers cannot trust others. The Cetronen, after all, wiped out our civilization."

Carrie said, "But now they've re-created you. They admitted to themselves, and to you, that they were wrong, and brought you back."

"May I and my people travel to your homeworld and wipe out your species?" Arda asked. "May we destroy all evidence of your civilization on that homeworld? May we be given only those records you find interesting?"

Carrie found her face flushing with anger. The Jenregar, after all, had only recently tried to do something similar. But she made herself grow calm. *Arda*, she thought, probably doesn't know a thing about what Earth's been through lately.

Arda's voice rumbled with greater force: "Then, centuries later, may we re-create your own people, so that we may tell ourselves that we are a moral species? And may we be amazed when you are less grateful, less satisfied with the circumstances of your return than we believe you should be?"

Carrie said to Arda, "All the same, you have returned, and that's to the Cetronen's credit. And it's a development that I believe much of Humanity would like to rejoice in, and share with Sungazers."

"'Much of Humanity?' Not all of it?"

"There are always those among us who disagree."

"Not among my people. Decisions are left to tribal leaders. In truth, there is very little to decide among my people. We nurture our young. We protect one another as the sun feeds us. From time to time, we move to new surroundings, to see what is over the next hill."

Both Marlow and Wait stood high in Costaguanan skies now, and though each was half the size of Earth's moon, they provided enough light for a Human, Sungazer, and Cetronen pair to see one another.

"My people have what you may think of as the equivalent of tribal leaders," Carrie said. "But they do not have absolute rule. Arda, you and I need to talk some more. But that will have to be after I consult with the other Humans on this planet."

"The Cetronen told us of your Human customs. They intrigue us. Do your consultations, then, and come back soon to tell us what is born of them."

———

Fortunately, although Green Town residents didn't allow their lives to revolve around communications tech, it was available if needed. Most families had at least one member equipped with a datalink, and most homes contained some sort of alert system. That's how Carrie was able to call an emergency town hall meeting that same night. She asked Col. Eisler to accompany her with only two lightly armed and unarmored Marines for security.

Carrie had only arrived on Costaguana hours before the Cetronen landed, and she'd had little opportunity to take in details of the local culture. Most residents of the planet were farmers, scientific researchers, and literary historians.

As she and the others approached the town hall, Carrie was struck by the homes constructed of wood and stone and the simple dress of their inhabitants.

In the town square, most merchants in their small shops were closing up for the night and outside vendors were securing their carts.

But these people aren't Luddites, Carrie thought, *and they don't let their "simple" lifestyle dominate their lives.* She knew many of these primitive-looking homes had food replicators and the latest medical nanotech inside. Living a simple life, most Human Costaguanans reasoned, didn't mean toiling so many hours that you didn't have time to spend with family or denying yourself the best healthcare.

One of the town leaders, a tall bearded man named Abraham Penzak, who was also an anthropology professor, met Carrie and Col. Eisler at a rear entrance to the hall. "Nearly the entire town is here," Penzak said. From the shadows at one side of the stage at one end of the large room, Carrie saw the crowd squeezing into every available chair and lining the walls. She saw farmers wearing sturdy, deeply soiled overalls. She saw strong, rough hands with dirt imbedded deeply under fingernails. Many of the women were dressed in clothing that didn't have to survive the same wear and tear as that worn out in the fields, but was still practical enough to do chores in.

Others, representing the more scholarly aspects of Costaguanan society, wore colorful caftans or tunics, and sandals.

Carrie glimpsed eager expressions, worried expressions, expressions that said these people were eager to know what dangers they might be about to face.

The undercurrent of conversations stilled as Penzak accompanied Carrie and Col. Eisler onstage and introduced them, then stood to one side. Carrie spoke first: "Most of you probably know by now of the native Costaguanans -- Sungazers, they call themselves -- who returned to this planet earlier today." She summarized the Sungazers' demands, concluding by saying, "We hope that they accept that Humanity is living here, too, and that they intend to accommodate us."

Penzak, standing just behind Carrie, was the first to speak up: "What if they decide not to accommodate us? Or, if they have several tribes, what if one wants to live in peace with us and another does not?"

Col. Eisler said, "That's why I'm here with my Marines. Now, the last thing we want is to see anyone hurt. But these Sungazers are not technological beings. We have more than enough personnel and equipment to make sure they can't attack anyone."

Penzak said, "Our grandparents came here to make a world that is, if not without conflict, then at least with much less conflict than other Human worlds. We aren't a paradise, but it's a place where most of us feel secure. Can you guarantee that we'll remain safe here in Green Town?"

"Professor Penzak, I know better than to guarantee anything in life. So far the Sungazers haven't shown any sign of hostility. But we have no way of knowing whether that might change."

Carrie said, "We'll let you know as much as we can as soon as we can. We're headed right back out to the Sungazers to see how much more we can learn about them."

That said, it took the better part of twenty minutes for Carrie and Col. Eisler to leave the hall, since it seemed half the town had followup questions that neither of them had answers to.

———

Then it was back to the nearby plain where eight Cetronen starcraft stood over dozens of groupings of Sungazers scattered among them. Costaguana's larger moon, called Wait, had climbed well above the horizon, with the smaller moon, Marlow, just peeking over. Their reflected light illuminated the underside of a broad bank of clouds coming in from the south.

Col. Eisler told half of his Marines to stand down for now, return to the shuttles, and get some food and sleep. He told Carrie, "I'll have to set up a schedule of watches if it looks like we're going to be here awhile. And tentative plans if the Sungazers go on the move or the Cetronen act up somehow."

"That's a lot to plan for," Carrie said. "Do you have enough people?"

"I guess I'll know when something happens."

"I'm glad I don't have your job."

Col. Eisler gave Carrie a wry grin. "At least while you're out there talking to them, I'll be back here where I have a chance at a clear shot."

"Damn. Didn't think of that part. Well, I'd best get on with it."

"Good luck."

Most of the Sungazers were sitting around in small groups, apparently just talking. *Uh, oh,* Carrie thought. *How the hell do I tell which one's Arda, especially with just moonlight to see by? I hate admitting to the stereotype of "they all look alike," but so far they do!*

As Carrie neared one group of Sungazers, however, Arda lifted his two-and-a-half meter frame and strode away from his group to meet Carrie. He said, "We will speak tonight, you and I. Night is the time when we Sungazers are most alive, when we tell stories of the divine, and how it is revealed within our young."

Carrie said, "I don't have any stories of the divine, Arda."

"Do you not have such faith?"

This isn't a topic I consider very often, Carrie thought. "I . . . think I might believe in some sort of God. I'm not certain of its nature. But tell me what's important to you. What are some of the stories Sungazers tell each other at night?"

Arda stood his full height and lifted his four-segmented arms high into the air. "We speak of the sun, which hides behind the world, until it arrives again to nourish us. We speak of our young ones, and the tragedy and glory that so many do not survive into adult years."

"If I may," Carrie asked, "why 'tragedy and glory?'"

Arda lowered his arms and looked at Carrie. "Tragedy because our young are fragile. They do not develop their wings for nearly a year after they are born. Our parents nourish them through umbilicals that connect to either parent as needed. Some do not survive that first year, never seek independence. Predators take others, despite our best efforts."

Arda paused, and his wings extended slightly and shuddered. Carrie wondered whether that a sign of extreme emotion for a Sungazer. Arda continued: "It is glory because we know that the young ones who die before they develop their wings die while still divine."

The last thing I want to get into, Carrie thought, *is Sungazer theology.* But she told Arda, "Knowing that must give you great comfort."

"Let me tell you more about our people. There is the story of the injured father trapped in the shade who kept his umbilical attached to his daughter for three days of feeding, sacrificing himself for his child. And the mother who was so distraught over the death of her son that she went off into a cave to die in the dark."

Other stories were of great sacrifice, such as individuals fighting herds of predators that threatened entire tribes. *None of these stories tell of Sungazer aggression against other tribes or other species,* Carrie realized. *No stories of war or conquest. It all adds up to a picture of a people who loves their children deeply, are used to coping with hardship, and would willingly endure loneliness and pain and the death of loved ones during their struggles.*

That makes them a lot like many Humans. It could be easy for much of Humanity to identify with Sungazers.

It could also mean Humanity and Sungazers might be equally stubborn, equally unwilling to compromise should a conflict arise between them.

Arda's stories were long, and plentiful. After one particularly lengthy story, Carrie told Arda, "We have to talk about what happens to the Humans who have made their homes here."

Arda spoke in the same calm, reasoned tone he'd used to relate his stories. "This is a Sungazer world. These are our lands."

"Some parts of this world are Human lands, and have been for generations. You can't go around taking property -- "

"The land does not belong to Humanity."

"Don't you understand the work that goes into making a family, making a home, working the land?"

"All Sungazers make families. We all care for the young. We have no need to make houses or work the land. If Humanity is so unsuited to Costaguana, it should leave."

"Arda, we need to figure some things out before someone gets hurt."

"Sungazers do not intend to harm anyone. We hope Humanity feels the same way."

By now the sun was about to rise, a faint presence in a misty sky. Arda told Carrie, "You must excuse me," and he and all the other Sungazers who had gathered together and spoken quietly the entire night arranged themselves into their neat rows, spreading their wings wide. The protective circle of other Sungazers surrounded them.

For a time, Carrie stood there and watched these larger-than-life, enigmatic beings as they began their regimen of soaking up sunlight. She couldn't decide whether she'd spent the whole night awake or living an extended dream. Arda had entertained her with Sungazer stories and folklore, revealing a rich history mostly preserved orally, a tradition not unlike many cultures among Earth Humans or Jupiter whales.

If these Sungazers are content to make this their life, Carrie thought, *then Humans can co-exist with them without a problem.*

Carrie headed back to the shuttle *Devries*, where she found Col. Eisler on the small command deck studying a holographic projection of a map showing the area between the Sungazers' location and that of Green Town. "So," she told him, "I guess you didn't get a lot of sleep either."

"Coffee helps," Col. Eisler said. He indicated the map. "I can figure out any number of strategies to keep the Sungazers from Green Town. They outnumber us, but we have the superior tech unless they've been holding back on us. But there's one big problem."

Carrie poured herself a cup of coffee. "Lemme guess. The Cetronen."

"Exactly. How badly do we want to start an interplanetary incident?"

"That was my thought even as those ships were landing."

"The big question," Col. Eisler said, "is how much force do we use? These Sungazers are big and imposing, but they don't seem to have any weapons." He shook his head. "Use of force questions give me a headache."

"Arda tells me the Sungazers don't want to hurt anyone. If he's telling the truth, we'll see just how far good intentions get us."

———

Carrie crawled into a narrow sleeping module to the rear of the shuttle. *I'm hungry,* she thought, *but too tired to get back up and fix something to eat. Sad.*

Tired as she was, though, her mind raced, and she knew it

would be difficult to get to sleep. She placed a somno patch on her arm and soon drifted away.

———

When the call came over her datalink, it took Carrie a moment to come to full awareness. "What -- what was that? Who is this?"

"Col. Eisler. You need to come out here, quick as you can."

Carrie rushed from the shuttle. She was actually grateful for the chilly afternoon that helped her wake up and focus. She immediately saw that many of the Sungazers had begun to move from their positions around the Cetronen ships. About a hundred of them made their way forward cautiously, their wings kept close to their bodies.

Col. Eisler's Marines, in turn, were giving ground, at least for now. Several hundred meters behind them stood one of several farms situated between them and Green Town.

Carrie couldn't discern a pattern in the way the Sungazers advanced. It didn't look as if they were considering the tactical advantages of a particular direction or whether they should march in a particular formation. They might be out for a leisurely stroll.

But it's mid-afternoon, Carrie thought. *This should be prime feeding time for them. What the hell are they doing?*

Carrie had thought having four segments to their legs would give them an awkward stride, like cubes she'd seen of Earthly giraffes, which always looked to her to be an instant away from a disastrous fall. Instead, she saw that the top knee came up slowly but surely, and the three segments beneath pivoted down and forward in a way more like a thoroughbred horse -- still fragile, but much more sure-footed and confident.

Their approach was maddeningly slow, however, and for

an instant Carrie wished they would move more quickly, so whatever was to happen would be done.

But that's stupid, she thought, *especially since we have a family farm just behind us. We need time. Time to think. Time to come up with a course of action.*

She found Col. Eisler positioned between the approaching Sungazers and his line of Marines. "The moment's about to come," the colonel said, "when we answer that most important question. I'd much rather you try to talk reason into them."

"Let me find Arda," Carrie said.

"I haven't been able to spot him. So far, I'm telling my Marines to keep calm, keep giving ground, and for god's sake not point their weapons at them."

Carrie went toward the line of Sungazers and stopped when she was about five meters from them.

Each of the Sungazers stopped, all at once.

"Is Arda with you?" she asked.

Several of the Sungazers closest to her regarded her, some with tilted heads as if they were trying to understand her, but none of them spoke.

Carrie had never received formal training in First Contact protocols, but she knew the temptation in a situation like this was to keep talking, even when the being you were speaking with couldn't understand you. But you never knew what words you might use that happened to be a curse word or fighting words in someone else's language, so sometimes it was best to remain mute.

Besides, having made the initial attempt, it was always best to see how the other person responded before you tried again.

The Sungazer closest to Carrie bent down slightly to regard her. His eyes were little more than slits, without eyelids or eyelashes.

After a moment, though, the Sungazer turned his back on

Carrie and for an instant she allowed herself to believe he was going to lead the others away again.

Instead, the other Sungazers gathered themselves around him. About half, including the one Carrie had spoken with, formed the now-familiar series of rows. The rest formed their protective circle.

Even though Carrie anticipated what happened next, it was still mesmerizing.

The Sungazer Carrie had spoken to, safe within the inner rows of Costaguanans, lifted his arms, extending his broad, green wings to their fullest extent, from the tips of his fingers down to his slender calves. The wings sprang into place with the same familiar sound Carrie used to hear when her grandmother would snap a sheet into place over a bed.

Carrie was fascinated by the complexity of the veins within the Costaguanans' wings. They were a lighter green than the wings, and she could swear they were pulsing slightly. As she strained to look more closely, she wondered if that pulsing was an optical illusion caused by a rapid, back-and-forth color change rather than actual movement. A visible response to chemical changes?

The Sungazers tilted their heads toward the heavens, but not directly toward the sun. Watching closely, Carrie saw the top and bottom edges of their already narrow eye sockets drew closer together until they met -- their species' way, she realized, of closing their eyes in the absence of lids. It gave them a squinty look that was almost comical.

Carrie walked back toward the line of Unity Marines. She'd never seen Colonel Eisler's features so grim. His posture was so stiff it looked as if his armor had frozen up on him. He asked Carrie, "Do you know what a hell of a mess we're in here?"

Carrie said, "I believe I do."

"What happens when these Sungazers advance upon this farmhouse? We have to protect Human lives and property."

"We don't know that the Costaguanans will turn violent. What if we wait and see what happens?"

"That's not sound military policy, Carrie. You don't let the other guy get in the first punch. But if they advance toward the house, do I only use minimum force? That puts my Marines at risk."

Carrie glanced over at the line of Marines, who were still standing with their weapons at the ready. She knew it was difficult to remain at the ready in full armor for hours at a time, not knowing whether the next moment would contain boredom or the adrenaline rush of sudden combat.

Colonel Eisler continued: "Or do we try to stun them? We don't know the appropriate setting for their species. We could end up injuring them. And despite what you may think, Carrie, I don't want that any more than you do, but Humans have been on Costaguana for almost thirty years. They have families here, traditions, a younger generation who's never been to another world."

"These beings *arose* here. They've been here for millennia."

Col. Eisler frowned. "No, Carrie, these beings are reverse-engineered from the beings who arose here. And the Cetronen only brought them here a day ago." He nodded toward the farmhouse behind them. "We need to talk to these people. Let them know what's going on."

"Do we *know* what's going on?"

"Not particularly. They still deserve to know what might be ahead of them."

Carrie and the colonel came up to the farmhouse from the rear. Carrie said, "See the farmer coming off his back porch? He's wondering what's happening, same as we are."

Col. Eisler cast a stern look toward Carrie. "Of course he is. It's his land."

"He also looks to have his own pulse rifle. Sometimes it's as important to negotiate with your own people as anyone else." Carrie made sure to hold her hand out in greeting right away. The man's handshake was firm, no-nonsense. He was tall, dark-skinned, with close-cropped hair. "Oliver Kariango," the man said.

"Carrie Molina. Unity Liaison. And this is Col. Norman Eisler."

Kariango looked past Carrie toward the edge of his property where the Sungazers stood. "You've got to do something," he said. "I don't want those . . . things coming onto my land. And I don't want those Marines fighting a war on it, either."

Carrie said, "Mr. Kariango, the best thing you can do is go back into your house. We're here to try to communicate with these beings. But if that doesn't work, you'd better leave the fighting to the Marines."

Col. Eisler said, "Perhaps if we walk with you back to your house? I understand what it's like. I wouldn't want strangers all over my land, either."

"I'd appreciate that, Colonel. And if you could try to explain this to me and my wife Jane, I'd be obliged."

As Col. Eisler started toward the farmhouse with Kariango, he turned and shot a raised-eyebrow look toward Carrie that told her he'd explain as much to the Kariangos as he could.

Oliver Kariango led them to the front of the house and opened the screen door to allow his visitors into the living room. All the furniture and decorations had the rough-hewn charm of having been created from raw materials, nothing replicated or manufactured. Jane Kariango, a slight woman in a well-worn, practical house dress, sat on a couch, hands folded, expectant.

Oliver Kariango asked, "May we offer you anything? Food, drink -- "

Carrie said, "No, thank you, sir."

Col. Eisler told him, "I'm fine, as well."

Jane Kariango's demeanor made up for her small size. "What can you do for us?" she asked sharply. "You've got to get those things off our land."

Carrie said, "Mrs. Kariango, those 'things' are intelligent beings. We're still in the First Contact phase with them. Some of them haven't had our language programmed into their datalinks. We have to ask you to be patient."

Jane Kariango said, "This can't go on. Our children are at our neighbor Arthea's house, and I'm not bringing them back as long as these . . . beings! . . . are out there."

"I understand your concern. But as far as we know, these Sungazers -- native Costaguanans -- "

Oliver Kariango interrupted. "We consider *ourselves* Costaguanans."

Col. Eisler gave Carrie a quick let-me-take-this glance and spoke up. "We're not saying you should consider yourselves anything else, sir. But we're trying to keep everyone safe here -- you, *and* the beings outside."

Carrie said, "The fact remains that their species was here before any Humans were."

Jane Kariango said, "I don't know why you're taking *their* side. You're supposed to take *Humans'* side."

"What I'm trying to do, ma'am, is resolve this peacefully. As I was saying, we have no evidence that the native Costaguanans are violent."

Oliver Kariango asked, "Then why are all those Marines out there?"

Carrie had to concede the point. "We're being cautious. But we can't force those beings off your property yet."

"Why not? Let them learn what it's like now that they're sharing the planet with Humans."

"Mr. Kariango, I appreciate that you acknowledge we're sharing the planet. Our intention is to make sure everyone understands that. I'd much rather be able to communicate to the Sungazers in words than by violence."

Jane Kariango, though clearly exasperated, asked, "What can we do to help?"

Carrie looked out the living room's wide front window toward the Marines and the natives. "I'd say it's good you've sent the children away. I'd gather anything irreplaceable -- family items, cubes, holos, that kind of thing."

Jane Kariango said, "The *house* is irreplaceable. We built it by hand."

Oliver Kariango shook a finger at Carrie. "You'd best make sure this gets done quickly. Or some people aren't going to be so polite anymore. They aren't going to be so interested in sharing."

Carrie bit back a sharp reply. Such anger, multiplied by hundreds of Human Costaguanans, could bring about disaster, but she understood its source. For her to speak against that anger now would only intensify it. "I'll do my best, Mr. Kariango."

Col. Eisler said, "And I'll assign a couple of my Marines specifically to look after your house. If you'll excuse us?"

Carrie and Col. Eisler left the farmhouse. The Sungazers continued to stand just off the Kariangos' property. As they approached the line of Marines, Carrie saw the previously missing Arda approaching from the opposite direction.

"I don't know if this is good or not," Carrie said.

Col. Eisler said, "I don't see a reason to be optimistic."

Arda stopped at a point equidistant from the mass of Sungazers and the Marine line. Carrie couldn't detect what emotions might lie behind those hooded eyes. She told him, "Your people are making a potentially dangerous move. They've given several Humans quite a scare. We can't allow that."

"You would commit violence to protect *things*?"

Colonel Eisler spoke up: "All my Marines have their weapons set to stun. We're not about to kill anyone if we can help it."

"Very well," Arda said. "If you do not wish to harm anyone, we will proceed."

Carrie backed up instinctively at the sight of a two-and-a-half meter living monolith advancing upon her. All of the Sungazers began to line up with Arda and move forward.

They all started moving in the same instant, Carrie thought. *How do they communicate that?*

Colonel Eisler said, "Move aside, Carrie. You're in our line of fire."

Carrie started walking perpendicular to the advancing Sungazers, telling Arda, "You've got to talk to us. We can't let things get out of hand."

"You say you do not lie, and that you do not wish to harm us. Is either of those things true?"

"We need to -- " Carrie's path intersected one of the advancing Sungazers, and when she struck his massive leg, her feet slipped out from under her. Arms flailing, she fell onto her back. Her breath *whooshed* out of her and for a moment she couldn't find the wherewithal to get up.

The Sungazers halted. Arda towered over her for a long moment. Then his thin, four-segmented arms reached down toward her, and all she could make out were his unreadable slit-like eyes and strong three-fingered hands that looked as if they were about to scoop her up.

A flash of light came from behind Carrie and she turned her face away from Arda and covered her head with her hands. Something large struck the earth, close enough to take her breath away again, then she heard Humans shouting and untranslated guttural Sungazer noises, as her datalink's translator failed to process so much input.

Even as the commotion died down, Carrie heard Col. Eisler still cursing. She got herself up on one knee and saw Arda's still form lying face down next to her.

Col. Eisler grabbed a med scanner from a Marine standing next to him and took a reading on Arda's body. The crestfallen look on his face told Carrie all she needed to know, but she had to ask anyway. "Is he -- "

"Yes. His heart stopped. From a stunner blast."

The other Sungazers mingled around behind Arda's body, their once neat line shattered into chaos.

"What the hell happened?" Carrie asked.

Col. Eisler handed the med scanner back to the Marine he'd taken it from, and stalked along his line of Marines toward one who was still pointing his pulse rifle at the space where Arda had been standing.

Carrie could only stare in numbed silence as around her came the sound of Sungazer wings flapping open, ready to receive nourishment from the sun.

Colonel Eisler snatched the Marine's weapon from him, then told him to remove his armor, which left him standing there in his skivvies in the chill day.

Colonel Eisler disassembled the Marine's weapon, examined its various parts, then reassembled it and handed it to another Marine. The cords of Eisler's neck stood out, he lifted himself up on the balls of his feet, and he put his face about four centimeters from Hardesty's face. As he addressed the Marine who had shot Arda, it was in tones Carrie associated with the toughest of drill instructors: "What the hell, Private Hardesty, did you think you were doing, firing without orders?"

Hardesty stood at stiff attention in his olive-drab shorts and T-shirt, looking not at his colonel but straight ahead. "I believed the Unity liaison was in trouble, SIR!"

"Are you saying my reflexes are too slow, Marine?"

"No, SIR!"

"Are you saying individual Marines make their own choices regarding use of force?"

"No, SIR!"

"Do you understand how badly you've fucked up?"

"Yes, SIR!"

"Report to your sergeant, who won't treat you as kindly as I have."

"Yes, sir. Thank you, sir." Hardesty left, not daring to give anyone, Carrie included, the slightest glance as he left, his hardened expression retaining what little dignity he still possessed.

Once Private Hardesty departed, Colonel Eisler's shoulders sagged. He took Carrie to one side, out of earshot of the other Marines. "Yes, I was rough on that boy. The sad part is, I was ready to give the fire order myself."

Carrie said, "You mean he jumped the gun by just an instant? Then why -- "

"Was I so rough? Because the next time I might *not* be about to give the order. *He* doesn't get to decide."

Carrie looked at the grouping of Sungazers, still in their formation of rows surrounded by their protective circle. "At least they didn't react violently. In fact, I can't tell that they reacted at all."

Col. Eisler said, "Maybe they're just building up strength before they move on us."

"I have to wonder why they made this initial move during the day at all. You'd think they'd want to spend as much time as they could soaking up energy."

"I don't know. Element of surprise, maybe? But I'm with you. I thought they'd move at night, if at all."

"I saw you looking at that Marine's pulse rifle. Was something wrong with it?"

"I was double-checking to see whether it malfunctioned somehow. But . . . no. It didn't."

"Which means even our stun settings kill Sungazers."

"It looks that way," Col. Eisler said. "Which could mean that unless we intend to commit mass murder, our regular weapons are useless."

"So now what do we do?"

"I'm not about to ask for permission to do an autopsy on Arda. I'm going to have a couple of my medics get as good a remote scan as they can -- pin down exactly what killed him. Then see if maybe we can change our pulse rifle settings so that we can actually stun a Sungazer instead of killing them."

"What happens if the Sungazers advance in the meantime?"

"We've got sticky-stuff we can shoot at them. Stop them in their tracks. I've got a few Marines trained in crowd-control techniques. Batons, bolos, nets, that kind of thing."

"Sounds kind of primitive."

"Hell, Carrie, if a stunner will kill them, I can't risk anything like tear gas or urp-spray. I can only try to restrain them."

"That'll have to do for now, I guess. Have you heard anything from the Unity? Any chance of reinforcements?"

"I think the Unity wishes this whole thing would just go

away. Costaguana isn't strategically important to us. And there aren't enough people living here for the diplomats to risk getting into a fight with the Cetronen. And I've got more immediate problems to worry about."

"Such as?"

"I can't keep these Marines on alert all day, every day indefinitely. I've got some reserves up with the *Kojima*, and I've got to start bringing them down and sending some of my current people back up. If we're going to be down here for any length of time, I need more than a shuttle for a command post and mess hall."

Carrie said, "If there's anything I can do -- "

"Just keep thinking. Give me any alternatives you come up with. And get some more rest, for God's sake. You're no good to anybody if you're exhausted."

"All right, Colonel, you convinced me. By the way, when was the last time *you* slept?"

"Oh, don't worry. Marines are issued sleep rations when they're needed."

Carrie only grunted in reply. She left him and was halfway to the shuttle *Devries* when she realized she had no idea whether Colonel Eisler had been joking or not.

————

Carrie curled up in one of the shuttle's sleeping modules again, dropped right off. It seemed only a moment later when she became vaguely aware of Col. Eisler's voice over her datalink yet again: "Carrie -- Carrie -- wake up!"

"Hmmm. . . . yeah?"

"Are you awake?"

"Yeah. Think so."

"Then get your ass over here to the Kariango farm. I need you."

"Now what?"

"It turns out the Sungazers had reinforcements inside the Cetronen ships. They've destroyed the Kariangos' farm."

———

At least I got a few hours sleep, Carrie thought as she trudged toward the Kariangos' farmhouse, or at least the foundation and debris that indicated where it once stood. Work lights Col. Eisler's men had situated all around the site illuminated the splintered timbers and fallen walls that were once the Kariango's home. Shattered pieces of furniture, torn strips of clothing, and the myriad other belongings that symbolize a family's life together were strewn across the landscape.

Just beyond that demolished home, however, two Sungazers were lying on the ground, trying to wriggle their way out of a tight netting that bound them. A third stood to one side, straining to pull his legs from two mounds of sticky material that kept him from taking another step.

Carrie spotted Col. Eisler and went to him. "They didn't give us any warning," he said. "These new Sungazers started marching out of those Cetronen ships. They started across the fields in back of the Kariango farm, bypassing my line of Marines. I caught them on sensors, started to redeploy -- but we were too late."

Carrie, remembering Oliver Kariango's pulse rifle, asked, "Did the Kariangos fight back?"

"They didn't. I don't know why, and I don't know what would've happened if they did. The Sungazers woke them up here in the middle of the night, demanded they leave their own home."

"And no one was hurt?"

"No, thank goodness. The Kariangos grabbed some belongings and ran to a neighbor's farm -- Arthea Yetter, the same woman who's been keeping their children. The last thing they saw was Sungazers tearing down their home and their barn."

Carrie indicated the Sungazers in the net and the one immobilized in sticky-stuff. "But you got these three. What happened to the others?"

"On their way to Green Town, it looks like."

"So you're going to have to engage them?"

Col. Eisler took off his helmet and rubbed his hand through his close-cropped hair. "Maybe not for a little bit. They're pretty slow. I did a rough time estimate. The sun should come up before they get to town. I hope they'll stop to soak up some sun."

"They moved toward the Kariango farm once before in the daytime."

"That's why I said 'hope' and not 'expect.' Oh, and we figured out what killed Arda. Basically, the stunner shorted out the electrical fields that accompany their speech. That started what the docs called a cascade effect throughout his body. Massive organ failure, including the heart."

"Damn. And what about tweaking the stunner settings?"

"I've got people working on that. Problem is, the only way to test it might be -- "

"To shoot another Sungazer?"

Col. Eisler said, "I hope it doesn't come to that."

"All right. I'm going to go see the Kariangos. They're going to be angry and scared, and . . . I'm afraid there are going to be more people like them soon. I have to know what we'll be coping with."

———

Arthea Yetter was a woman in her sixties who opened her front door to Carrie and immediately scowled at her. "I'm not sure why I should let you into my house," she said.

"I'm here to help," Carrie told her. The door opened onto Yetter's living room, and Carrie could see the Kariangos and their two children sitting on a long couch. The Kariangos' son, Martin, looked to be about six years old, their daughter Marie perhaps a couple of years younger.

Oliver Kariango got up from the couch and pointed an accusing finger at Carrie. "Our house is *gone*. Destroyed by these creatures. We'll never have it back."

Carrie said, "You can replicate -- "

"You can't replicate the sweat we put into that home. You can't bring back the scratches we made in one of the doorways to see how much taller the children were each year. There was a stain on the floorboards in the laundry room where the cat had kittens one year. We could never get it up completely. Can you bring that back?"

"Mr. Kariango, I understand the sentimental value those things have for you -- "

Jane Kariango rose to stand next to her husband. "It's more than sentiment," she said. "It's our *lives*. Those scratches, that stain, they're how we know we lived in that house. They're how we marked the days. Before that, it was building the house itself. It was before the children came, and it took months, while Oliver and I lived in tents and slept on cots. You may wonder why we would undergo such hardships, but to us they weren't hardships, they were how we showed love for the land and love for the children, our children, even before they were born. Is there any way in hell you can even *begin* to understand that?"

Carrie steeled herself: "I'm not here to trade tragedies with you or see who's suffered the most. But my mother died of the Monaco Virus over twenty years ago. A madman killed my sister. And my father was tortured and killed at the hands of the Jenregar. So disagree with me if you want, hate me if you want, but don't think it's because I've never had anything tragic happen in my life."

Jane Kariango's expression softened only slightly. She said, "I'd never wish such things on anyone."

Carrie said, "You've lost your home, and I don't want anyone else to go through that. But one of the Sungazers, Arda, died when we tried to stun him. We're trying to figure out how to stop them without killing them."

Oliver Kariango started to speak, but his wife touched him on the arm and he stayed silent. Jane Kariango told Carrie, "You have to decide who you're here to represent. Now, I don't want any more killing if we can help it. But the plain fact of it is that we may not be *able* to help it. And if you don't help the Humans here, who are you helping?"

Carrie looked at Jane Kariango, and saw a slight woman wearing a simple dress and a worn coat, a woman who'd worked hard to create a life for herself and her family and saw that life being torn from her. Carrie told her, "Mrs. Kariango, I have to look beyond Costaguana. I represent the Earth Unity. There are Galactic species who haven't forgotten the Great Human War, who still mistrust us. Arda died at Humanity's hands. Never mind that it was the act of a single scared individual. What if it happens again and again, a dozen times or more?"

Oliver Kariango said, "I don't give a *damn* what happens to these Sungazers. *That's* something you'd better learn, and quick!"

Jane Kariango's arms went around her husband, and she

caressed his cheek and spoke soft words to him, trying to praise him and calm him at the same time.

Carrie could only say, "I have to get back to work. Good luck to you both."

Oliver Kariango said, "I suspect, Carrie, that you hold much of our luck in your hands."

As Carrie left Arthea Yetter's house, the first rays of the rising sun silhouetted the Cetronen ships that remained at their landing site, as well as the many Sungazers that were still gathered around them.

She touched behind her left ear. "Col. Eisler, what are the Sungazers headed toward Green Town doing?"

Carrie could hear the relief in the colonel's voice: "They've stopped their advance, at least for now," he said.

"Here's hoping we've at least got the rest of today's daylight hours to come up with a new plan."

"That plan will have to be a lot more extensive than you think."

"Why's that?"

"I was waiting for you to finish talking to the Kariangos so I could tell you. The Cetronen are stepping in. We have a week to evacuate the planet."

"Goddam. Where are you now?"

"Back aboard *Devries*."

"I'll be right there."

As Carrie started back toward the shuttle, though, she stopped cold as she realized the silhouettes of the Cetronen craft were beginning to rise. One by one, the eight ships ascended into the morning skies, the roaring of their gravitic drives slowly fading. Carrie stood transfixed for a time, hands at her sides, preternaturally aware of the blood pulsing at her neck, of her ragged breathing, and of the shame she felt as she wished she were blinking back tears of rage rather than of fear. She realized, *They've dropped off all the remaining Sungazers, so they don't have any reason to stay.*

She touched behind her left ear. "This is Carrie Molina to Ambassador Golareg."

No response.

"Ambassador Golareg, do you copy?"

Still silence. And she realized, *Now the only negotiations I have left to perform are with my own people.*

————

Carrie found Col. Eisler aboard *Devries* examining another holographic projection, this one of the various paths of the Cetronen ships as they boosted toward orbit. "Look at that," the colonel said, indicating the holo. "They're taking up positions all around the planet."

Carrie nodded. "In case the Unity decides to defend us."

The holo disappeared at Col. Eisler's angry gesture. "They don't have to worry about that. Oh, they're sending several starcraft -- they could actually be here within a few hours -- but it's for an evacuation."

"So we force thousands of Humans to leave the world they've known for generations," Carrie said. "And these evacuation ships sure got here in a a hurry. This must've been the plan all along, and they didn't tell us." Stating it out loud made the more real somehow, made the choices in front of her stand out in stark relief in her mind.

Col. Eisler said. "The Unity isn't about to take on a conflict with the Cetronen over Costaguana. And there's a dirty word that's caused considerable panic back home, as well. Genocide."

"Yeah. I should've realized that."

"We destroyed millions of Jenregar back on Earth -- maybe

a good proportion of the entire species. It was self-defense. We had to do it. But that word got thrown around a lot afterwards. The Unity heard it in connection with the Sungazers and panicked."

"All right, then. I guess it's time for another town hall meeting."

———

Carrie called on Abraham Penzak to get the word out about the meeting, and he came through for her -- the hall was even more crowded than before.

The mood was more somber than earlier, as well. Carrie heard only muted conversations as she entered the hall, which stilled as people saw her arrive. Parents shushed children; everyone moved to clear a space for Carrie as she moved toward the small stage.

She found Penzak, shook his hand, and thanked him for arranging the meeting on such short notice. The man was wearing his usual caftan and sandals, but his silent nod to Carrie and the way he kept rubbing his beard told her his usual serenity was lacking.

Looking out into the crowd of people before her, Carrie saw a presence that hadn't been there the previous time -- the Kariango family. She recognized Oliver's tall, lanky frame standing next to his wife Jane's slight form. Standing in front of them were the Kariango children.

Might as well jump right in, Carrie thought. "Thanks to everyone for coming here on such short notice. I'll get right to the point. The Unity has decided that all Humans on Costaguana will have to be evacuated."

Carrie was ready to flinch, as she expected an immediate uproar, dozens of voices making loud protests. Instead, the

Green Town residents simply stared. Some exchanged shocked looks, a few murmured to the person next to them, but most sat silently and continued to give Carrie their full attention.

She continued: "The Sungazers don't want Humanity here, and we can't protect ourselves effectively against them without killing them in large numbers. Several starcraft are on the way here to take everyone away."

Penzak asked, "Isn't it the Unity's responsibility to protect us from this kind of threat?"

Carrie took a deep breath. "Yes, it is. But in this case, we don't see a way to come out a winner. We might have to commit something close to genocide against the Sungazers. Not to mention the possibility of a conflict with the Cetronen if we do that. If this planet turns into a battleground, Humans could die in massive numbers and many of your communities could be leveled."

Now dozens of voices rose at once, and Carrie held up her hands to try to quiet the crowd. "I'm afraid there isn't time for a lot of debate," she said. "The Unity starcraft are expected here within hours."

Oliver Kariango's voice rose above everyone else's. "You mean to take everyone who *wants* to go!"

Carrie faced him. "This can't be voluntary. We won't leave people to die. You need to get ready to leave."

"And you won't help us fight. You're cowards!" Other voices rose up in support of Kariango's outburst.

Exactly what I feared, Carrie thought. *It only takes that one determined voice to bind a crowd of people together against a common enemy.*

In this case, me.

Jane Kariango spread her arms wide to the crowd. "Everyone who's with us, clap and stomp!" And she started clapping her hands.

Carrie tried to speak, but was drowned out by the crowd's

clapping. The floor shook with their stomping. Some of the smaller children covered their ears against the din, others clapped loud as they could and even began dancing to the rhythm.

The heat in the room was becoming oppressive, and Carrie felt sweat beads forming on her forehead. If she looked from side to side, she started feeling dizzy. *I've got to get out of here,* she thought. *There's nothing more I can say that these people will listen to.*

She started through the crowd, excusing herself to those she pressed past. "My husband was right," Jane Kariango shouted over the din. "She *is* a coward, like all those Unity Earthers."

Carrie was tempted to whip around and challenge Mrs. Kariango on that point, and especially on her use of language, but decided that wouldn't help her cause a bit. The crowd continued chanting as Carrie left the town hall to head back toward *Devries*.

———

Carrie spent the next several hours aboard the shuttle working with Col. Eisler on an evacuation plan. A holographic representation of Green Town floated before them in the cramped confines of the shuttle's command deck. Carrie asked, "So just how many Unity ships are on the way?"

"Four," Col. Eisler said. "Exploratory ships *Montana, Azure Dragon,* and *Black Tortoise.* And *Erasmus.* That's a personnel transport."

"It's going to be pretty tight lodgings."

"It's the better part of a week back to Earth. They'll get by."

"It'll be quite a transition for some of these people who've never even been to Earth. Especially since they're being dropped right down into the recovery effort there."

"These are people who know how to cope with adversity," Col. Eisler said. "They'll get by." Then the colonel got a distracted look and Carrie realized he was listening to an incoming datalink message.

Col. Eisler looked directly at Carrie and said, "We've got to head toward Green Town."

"What's happening?"

"Some of them aren't getting ready to evacuate. They're getting ready to fight."

———

Carrie and Col. Eisler rushed out of the *Devries* and past the site of the demolished Kariango house. The entire time, the colonel barked orders through his datalink to move Marines away from their duties monitoring Sungazers so they could intercept what looked like a large percentage of the population of Green Town.

Col. Eisler told Carrie, "It looks like some of these people are armed. A few pulse rifles and pistols. Others with just clubs or hammers."

"We didn't come here to fight our own people."

"Don't worry, Carrie. At least we can stun them. And believe me, I won't hesitate to give that order. And remember my people are wearing armor and they aren't."

A line of Marines, about two dozen of them, stood between the Sungazers who'd halted their advance after they'd destroyed the Kariangos' home and the approaching towns-people. Carrie squinted through a mass of narrow, intertwined trunks of braidwood trees, and could see a great many people approaching down a single narrow path.

The Sungazers who formed the protective circle around those who were soaking in the sun's energy turned in the direction of the approaching Humans. They stood at the ready, several with fists clenched as if preparing for a boxing match. The circle broke up as several Sungazers came around as additional forces.

The Sungazers in the middle remained standing with their wings spread, but turned their heads toward the Humans.

Col. Eisler took his place at the head of the line of Marines. "These townspeople outnumber us about three to one. But they get one warning. We tell them to stop. If they don't stop, we fire on stunner setting, wide beam. Only at my command!"

As the lead Humans emerged from within the stand of braidwood trees, Col. Eisler spoke through his wrist mic: "You need to return to your homes and get ready to be evacuated. If you come any closer, we *will* stun you!"

The mass of people stopped. Carrie recognized Abraham Penzak among them. Penzak was unarmed, but he spoke briefly to Oliver Kariango, who was carrying his pulse rifle. Then Penzak stepped out from among the others and approached Col. Eisler. Carrie stepped forward to join them.

Penzak looked past Eisler and Carrie, getting a good look at the Sungazers. "This is the first I've seen them up close," he said. He looked at Col. Eisler and said, "All my people want is to talk to these . . . Sungazers."

Col. Eisler said, "We're not here to negotiate. That time is past. And I see some of your people still getting closer. This isn't something we talk over."

The colonel tilted his head in such a way that Carrie knew he was getting another datalink update. He told Penzak, "By the way, our sensors also detected the other group of your people trying to flank us. Head back toward your homes or we'll stun the lot of you where you stand."

From among the group of townspeople, Oliver Kariango let out a loud scream and raised his pulse rifle.

"Fire," Col. Eisler said, with a calm and matter-of-factness that surprised Carrie.

Several of the Marines got shots off before Kariango could fire. He fell to the ground.

"He's not hurt," Col. Eisler told Penzak. "But think of what's best for your people. I know this is a difficult moment for you. Let your people leave here with some dignity. Do you really want their families and friends seeing us bringing their unconscious bodies back into town?"

Penzak stared at Col. Eisler with a fiery hatred. He turned that stare onto the Sungazers for a long moment. Then, without a word, he marched back toward the other townspeople. After a heated discussion among them, a couple people lifted Oliver Kariango's unconscious form between them and they and all the rest headed back in the direction of Green Town.

———

Two nights later, various Unity shuttles began landing in the same dusty plain the Cetronen craft had used earlier.

Within minutes, Carrie was guiding people toward the shuttles *Judith* and *Missouri*, out of the archeological ship *Montana*. Still to come were shuttles from the starcraft *Azure Dragon* and *Black Tortoise*. "Come along folks," Carrie said as she waved along the line of people filing past her. Those two shuttles could only hold a few dozen people apiece, but after several trips, the *Montana's* cargo hold would be packed.

Overhead, visible even against the glow of the lighted

pathways and landing areas, shone stars beyond counting. Some of those stars *moved* and Carrie wondered which of them were Cetronen craft and which were the Unity ships.

Col. Eisler came up to Carrie as the last people assigned to *Judith* and *Missouri* for this trip climbed aboard. "With any luck," he said, "by tomorrow they'll all be gone. Although we've had to drag some out literally kicking and screaming."

Carrie wiped dust from her face. "So the Sungazers get a second chance. I hope they make the most of it." She held her hands against her ears against the scream of gravitics as the personnel transport craft *Erasmus* gingerly settled onto the surface of the planet. It could hold a couple hundred people all on its own, and, being self-contained rather than a shuttle, could boost directly toward Earth or one of its orbital habitats.

"I know this hasn't been the most satisfying of outcomes," Col. Eisler said. "But always remember you helped save both the Humans who lived here *and* the Sungazers. That's no small feat."

Carrie managed a small smile. "I guess that'll have to do."

"I'm headed back to the *Devries*. We won't take off until everyone else is gone. I'll see you back there."

Now townspeople streamed toward *Erasmus*. The wide entry doors at its rear slid apart and they streamed into what was normally a cargo bay, carrying as many of their belongings as they could. The Marines, for their part, tried to hold onto their patience as they quietly informed individual refugees that they couldn't allow them to carry on their favorite chair, or a bicycle, or in one case, a piano on wheels. Carrie wondered how it had survived the trip over Green Town's cobblestone streets and through the woods.

Then Carrie's breath caught as she saw a man, a woman, and a swiftly chattering boy and girl standing in line.

The Kariangos.

Carrie approached them and said, "I'm sorry at how this all turned out."

Jane Kariango's angry glance insisted, *No you're not.* Carrie ignored it.

The children, Martin and Marie, turned quiet; they knew adults were talking seriously in a way they didn't quite understand, and Carrie recognized the combination of curiosity and apprehension that silenced them. She hoped not to create a scene here, didn't wanted the intensely personal to burst out into the open, in front of staff and strangers alike, but she could see that was another wish about to be shattered.

Oliver Kariango said, "We're losing a world, Carrie. Maybe someday you'll know what that's like."

Carrie realized Oliver, Jane, and the children were waiting for her to answer, and she was tempted to pour out all those those complex and conflicting thoughts and emotions that had flashed through her consciousness here amid this tragedy that was still unfolding across the Costaguanan landscape and in its skies.

No, she thought. *There's been too much animosity, too much high emotion already. Why add to it?*

Jane spoke up, and this time her gaze met Carrie's defiantly, and her tone was challenging: "Come along, Oliver. She'll never know. She's privileged. She's an *Earther*." Jane walked toward the evac craft without a backward glance.

Oliver Kariango didn't even glance at Carrie as he herded the children along to catch up to Jane.

Carrie started back toward the shuttle *Devries*. As she neared it, she saw in the distance, illuminated by the faint reflected light from Costaguana's moons, a single row of Sungazers standing next to the ruins of the Kariango home, still as statues.

A Request From the Author

If you enjoyed KAYONGA'S DECISION, please consider giving it an honest review on Amazon. It's the best thing you can do to help out an author whose work you like!

About the Author

Dave Creek is the author of the novels ALL HUMAN THINGS, CHANDA'S AWAKENING, and SOME DISTANT SHORE, novellas TRANQUILITY and THE SILENT SENTINELS, and short story collections A GLIMPSE OF SPLENDOR and THE HUMAN EQUATIONS.

He's also published the Great Human War trilogy, including A CROWD OF STARS (2016 Imadjinn Award winner), THE FALLEN SUN, and THE UNMOVING STARS (2018 Imadjinn Award winner).

Dave also edited TRAJECTORIES, an anthology of stories about space exploration and its many challenges, and is the author of MARS ABIDES: RAY BRADBURY'S JOURNEYS TO THE RED PLANET, a non-fiction look at Bradbury's Martian stories.

His short stories have appeared in ANALOG SCIENCE FICTION AND FACT, AMAZING STORIES, and APEX magazines, and the anthologies FAR ORBIT APOGEE, TOUCHING THE FACE OF THE COSMOS, and DYSTOPIAN EXPRESS. He's also been published in the Russian SF magazine ESLI and China's SCIENCE FICTION WORLD.

In the "real world," Dave is a retired television news producer.

Dave lives in Louisville with his wife Dana, son Andy, Corgi/Jack Russell Terrier mix Ziggy Stardawg, and poly-dactyl cat Hemmie.

Stay in Touch With Dave

E-mail
  dave@davecreek.com

Website:
  http://www.davecreek.com

Facebook:
  https://www.facebook.com/davecreek

Twitter:
  @DaveCreek

www.ingramcontent.com/pod-product-compliance
Lightning Source LLC
Chambersburg PA
CBHW060922250626
47159CB00008B/3114